7/20

D0187027

RANDOM HOUSE

LARGE PRINT

ALSO BY ALEXANDER McCALL SMITH
AVAILABLE FROM
RANDOM HOUSE LARGE PRINT

The Talented Mr. Varg
The Second-Worst Restaurant in France
The Department of Sensitive Crimes
The Quiet Side of Passion
My Italian Bulldozer
The No. 1 Ladies' Detective Agency

THE GEOMETRY OF
HOLDING HANDS

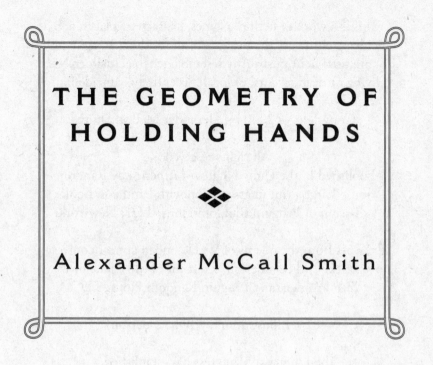

THE GEOMETRY OF HOLDING HANDS

Alexander McCall Smith

RANDOM HOUSE
LARGE PRINT

This is a work of fiction. Names, characters, places, and incidents either are the product of the author's imagination or are used fictitiously. Any resemblance to actual persons, living or dead, events, or locales is entirely coincidental.

Copyright © 2020 by Alexander McCall Smith

All rights reserved.

Published in the United States of America by Random House Large Print in association with Pantheon Books, a division of Penguin Random House LLC, New York.

Excerpts from the poems of W. H. Auden appear courtesy of Edward Mendelson, Executor of the Estate of W. H. Auden, and Penguin Random House LLC.

Cover illustration by Bill Sanderson

The Library of Congress has established a Cataloging-in-Publication record for this title.

ISBN: 978-0-593-21247-9

www.penguinrandomhouse.com/large-print-format-books

FIRST LARGE PRINT EDITION

Printed in the United States of America

10 9 8 7 6 5 4 3 2 1

This Large Print edition published in accord with the standards of the N.A.V.H.

This book is for Roma and Michael Menlowe.

THE GEOMETRY OF
HOLDING HANDS

CHAPTER ONE

WE DESERVE IT, don't we?" said Isabel Dalhousie, half in jest—but only half.

On the other side of the kitchen table, her husband, Jamie—whom she still thought of as her lover, as he thought of her too—was engaged in feeding their younger son, Magnus, a mixture of boiled egg and yoghurt. It was an unlikely dish, not one to be found in any cookbook of children's food, but one that Magnus clearly enjoyed, at least judging by the way he waved his arms with delight whenever it was offered to him. Magnus had developed a habit of waving his arms that Jamie, in particular, found endearing. "He's destined to be a conductor," he announced proudly.

"That's the first sign. Daniel Barenboim must have waved his arms exactly like that when he was a baby."

"Be careful what you wish for," Isabel had cautioned. "Would you want Magnus to grow into Toscanini?"

Jamie laughed. As a professional musician, he had experienced his fair share of difficult and irascible conductors. Conductors could be bullies and fly into rages. "Perhaps not," he said. "Unless that's what he wanted." He looked intently at Magnus, who stared back at him. "Would you like to be like Arturo Toscanini, my wee darling?"

Magnus transferred his gaze to the bowl from which his father had been feeding him.

"I read that as a no," he said.

"Grub first, then music," said Isabel. "To parody Brecht."

Jamie picked up a spoon. He had stumbled upon the combination by mistake, when he had inadvertently emptied a carton of yoghurt into a bowl already containing chopped-up boiled egg. "I discovered it in the same way in which Sir Alexander Fleming discovered penicillin," he said. "He left a Petri dish on a windowsill, didn't he? And in floated the mould. Serendipity, I think they call it."

Now, as the last remnants of **œuf au yaourt,** as he called it, was scraped off the side of the bowl and offered to Magnus, Jamie thought about Isabel's question. They had been talking about their planned evening out, and Isabel, who tended to engage in moral self-examination in circumstances in which others would not bother, was now wondering about how they might justify a night out at an expensive restaurant.

Jamie looked across the table and grinned. "Are you worried about spending the money?" he asked. "This place . . . what's it called?"

"Casa Trimalchio . . . I think." She hesitated. "It made me think of **Trimalchio's Feast,** of course. Petronius, the **Satyricon.** Remember?"

Jamie shook his head. His classical education had stopped when he was sixteen, when the school's Latin teacher had died unexpectedly and had been replaced by a teacher of geography. "I never did Petronius," he said. "We did a bit of Ovid and Caesar's **De Bello Gallico,** which was really boring. **Gallia in tres partes divisa est . . .** I remember that bit.

Gaul is divided into three parts. God, Caesar was a bore." He remembered something else. "And a bit of Horace. Not much, but a few of his Odes. I liked him. He would never have divided Gaul into three parts. And then that was that. No Greek at all. I don't have a word of Greek, I'm afraid. Not one."

"Neither do I," said Isabel. "And yet does that stop me expressing views on Aristotle? Or Plato, while I'm about it? Not to mention the Stoics?" She laughed. "Aren't we a pair? Completely Greek-less." But then she thought: **Ethos, logos, akrasia**—she was full of Greek without knowing it, just like Molière's M. Jourdain, who discovered that he had been speaking prose for forty years without knowing it.

Jamie said, "So it's called Casa Trimalchio. I think I read a review in the **Scotsman.**"

Isabel had read it too. "They liked it. That's why I chose it."

He suddenly thought of Horace again. "Why did I like Horace?"

Isabel shrugged. "He was pleased with life. He liked to write about farms and bee-keeping and drinking wine with friends. He was that sort of poet."

"Like your W. H. Auden?"

"A bit. Auden had his Horatian moments. I think of 'In Praise of Limestone' in that light."

Jamie continued, "Horace wrote something that made our Latin teacher get hot under the collar. Blow a fuse."

"And mix a metaphor," muttered Isabel.

"I remember it distinctly," said Jamie. "Horace writes somewhere **Dulce et decorum est pro patria mori**—it's a sweet and noble thing to die for your country. And Mr. Henderson—he was the Latin teacher—shook his head and went red. He said, 'That, boys, is perfect nonsense. It isn't. It just isn't. Die for a cause, but not for a country. And even then, it's not sweet. It's tragic.'"

"Wilfred Owen would have agreed with him."

Jamie knew about that. "Ah, Britten's **War Requiem.** That's Owen, isn't it? There are those utterly bleak lines, **What passing-bells for these who die as cattle? Only the monstrous anger of the guns . . .** I was fourteen when I heard that for the first time. I couldn't believe it. It struck me as so sad. I was told that he was writing about eighteen-year-olds and that really struck me."

"I can imagine." She could; she had seen a photograph of him at about that age and it had tugged at her heart: she saw in him the fragile beauty that can flower in boys at that stage and then coarsens as they get older, although in his case it had not—it had persisted. There was something about that somewhere in Shakespeare's **Sonnets,** but she would not embarrass Jamie by mentioning it. He was indifferent to the way he looked, which was half his charm. People who were aware of their good looks could be narcissistic and precious, and that, curiously enough, was a form of ugliness. Jamie never looked in the mirror and had to be told when it was time to go to the hairdresser.

He reminded her that she had asked about Casa Trimalchio and whether they deserved their reservation there. "You don't have to worry all that much about money, Isabel," he said. "I know you don't throw it around—or talk about it. But it is there, isn't it? We're not exactly on the breadline."

She liked it when he said **we** in this context. Isabel had said from the beginning of their marriage that everything she had was his too—and she meant it. He, however, had been reluctant to dip into their joint bank account in any way, preferring to rely on the much smaller balance he kept in an old-fashioned savings account. It was into this account that his earnings as a musician and music teacher were paid—not much, he cheerfully pointed out, but enough to provide him with sufficient pocket money. The big bills—the expenses of running the house, Grace's salary, insurance payments, the garage bills for the green Swedish car and so on—all these were paid by Isabel.

"I know I don't have to worry," she conceded. "But I do. I don't worry about not having enough—I worry about the whole idea of spending money I didn't earn. You earn every penny of yours—I wish I could say the same."

"You work hard," he pointed out. "You edit the **Review.** You deal with all those

prima donna authors. Lettuce and that creepy Christopher . . ."

"Dove." He **was** creepy. It was an apt word for Dr. Christopher Dove. And Professor Lettuce, if not creepy in quite the same way as Christopher Dove, still seemed ridiculous. Isabel pictured him in all his self-importance. How might one describe Professor Lettuce? Perhaps no other word was necessary because his name—Lettuce—was ridiculous enough. Professor Robert Lettuce—how could one not smile at that? And yet making fun of another's name was simply childish—she reminded herself of that—even if there were names that seemed to invite such a response. There were people in Scotland called Smellie, an old Scottish name and one that many Smellies still bore with pride—defiance, even. Or there were those English names, mostly originally from Lancashire, she understood, like Sidebottom and Winterbottom. People of that name must as children have become hardened to the smirks of others, although how many of them must have yearned to wake up one morning as simple Sides or unremarkable Winters? She put thoughts of names out of her mind and listened instead to what Jamie was about to say about the morality, or otherwise, of inherited assets.

"You work pretty hard," Jamie continued, "and so, quite frankly, I don't see why you should feel guilty. What you're doing is using money from those investments—that trust over there—you're using that money to pay yourself for the work that the **Review** could never pay you for."

She looked doubtful. "I wish I could really see it that way."

"You could," he said. "Stop beating yourself up over being financially comfortable. That family of yours over in Alabama, or Louisiana, or wherever it was, worked hard for it. Now it's passed on to you. And you're using it well."

"Going out to dinner at expensive restaurants?"

Jamie shook his head in frustration. "When did we last do that? Come on, tell me when we last went out to dinner somewhere expensive."

"I can't remember," she replied, then hazarded a guess: "A couple of months ago?"

"Well, there you are."

GRACE HAD AGREED to do the babysitting. She had been Isabel's housekeeper, having more or less come with the house when Isabel had inherited it from her father. Grace had looked after him after the death of Isabel's mother—her "sainted American mother" as Isabel called her—and she regarded it as part of the natural order of things that she should continue in her post when Isabel eventually took over. Isabel demurred, but Grace had quietly taken on everything from cleaning to ordering groceries. When the children had arrived, she had assumed the additional role of nurse and nanny, washing, changing and feeding Charlie and Magnus with brisk efficiency. The boys loved her, although they both knew that Grace was inherently more difficult to manipulate than either of their parents. "Children can sense a pushover," Grace said, adding hurriedly, "not that I'm saying that either you or Jamie is that. Heavens, no. But they can tell who is going to let them get away with things, little devils."

Grace arrived early that evening. Magnus

was already asleep, but Charlie, being older, was on a half-hour extension, which would give him the chance to have his bedtime story read by Grace.

"You concentrate on getting into your finery," she said to Jamie. "I'll do the story."

Jamie accepted her offer. "He's been looking forward to that. There's a new book from the Morningside Library. Isabel got it today. It's about a boy who wants to wear a dress."

Grace was unsurprised. "Little boys sometimes want to dress like girls. My older cousin's son—the one who lived over in Lochgelly—he was like that. He was always putting on his sister's dresses. And . . ."

Jamie waited. Grace, although single herself, had a wide extended family, and usually had a relative whose example could illustrate any proposition. "And?" he prompted. He was not sure that this story would end well; Lochgelly, once a coal-mining town, was no place for a sensitive boy to live.

"He joined the army. He did pretty well. He's still in it."

"A Highland regiment?" asked Jamie. "They wear kilts."

Grace smiled. "No, the Royal Marines, actually."

"Ah."

"He's a sergeant now. He was based at Redford Barracks until a few months ago. Now he's with the Gurkhas somewhere."

Jamie raised an eyebrow.

"So you see, you can't tell," Grace concluded. "People should be able to do their thing, shouldn't they?"

"Of course," said Jamie. But he wondered about the cousin; he wondered whether he had been encouraged to make himself tough— and had overdone it. The Royal Marines did the job they had to do very well, but did they have to be **quite** so tough? Were the ranks of these regiments full of people who were trying to prove something to others, or even to themselves?

On impulse, Jamie said, "Do you think the army might try to be a little bit more in touch with its feminine side?"

Grace stared at him reproachfully. "Lots of women are in the army these days," she said. "And why not?"

Jamie nodded. "And a good thing too. I was

thinking about the men. All that shouting and bellowing and walking about in that rather stiff way. Why? Why not walk normally?"

"It's called marching," said Grace. "That's what soldiers do."

Grace went upstairs and relieved Isabel, who was trying to settle an excited Charlie in his room. Half an hour later she came downstairs, to find Jamie pouring a glass of New Zealand white wine for Isabel. They had both made an effort with their outfits, and Grace complimented them. She liked Jamie's blazer, she said. "A double-breasted jacket always suits a man. Unless he's too stout. Which you're not, of course."

Jamie thanked her and offered to pour her a glass of wine. Grace declined. "I've brought a book," she said. "And if I have a glass of wine I'll doze off in minutes. It always happens."

Jamie glanced at the book that Grace had brought in a see-through plastic bag. He could just make out the title: **Beyond the Beyond.** "Good?" he asked.

"Better than that library book," she answered, casting her eyes upstairs.

"Did he not enjoy it?" asked Isabel.

"No," said Grace. "We got to the second page and he said, 'Why does that boy want to wear a dress? He's not a girl.'"

Isabel smiled. "And so?"

"He asked for something different," said Grace. "He wanted that book about the dog who saves a train."

Jamie burst out laughing. "He might not be ready for the message just yet."

"Any boy would prefer to read about dogs who save trains," said Grace. "It's what boys like."

"Oh well," said Jamie. He pointed to Grace's bag. "**Beyond the Beyond**? Beyond as in . . . the other side?"

They were used to Grace's references to the other side. She was a regular attender at a spiritualist centre in the West End of Edinburgh and often told them about the seances and talks that took place there.

She nodded in answer to Jamie's question. "It's an interesting book," she said. "The author came to give a talk last week. He sold copies afterwards. That one's signed."

"What's it about?" asked Jamie.

"I'm not very far into it," Grace replied. "It's really his life story, I suppose. About how he became a medium and about some of the people he helped." She paused. "He knew when he was only seven or eight, you know. He lived up on one of the Hebrides— Mull, in fact. His father was the skipper of a fishing boat. He said that he predicted when his father would get a good catch and when the fish would be somewhere else altogether. And the weather. He had a premonition of a storm and warned his father not to go out."

"Perhaps he saw the weather report," Isabel suggested. "Meteorologists can be quite fey." She used the Scots word for one with clairvoyant powers.

Grace frowned. "I know you don't believe—"

"Isabel's only joking," Jamie said quickly. And to Isabel he said, "Remember what Hamlet said: 'There are more things in Heaven and Earth, Horatio, than are dreamt of in your philosophy . . .'"

"Yes," said Grace, slightly disapprovingly. "People should remember that." She looked at her watch. "Hadn't you better go? You said you were booked for eight."

"Yes, we are," said Jamie. "I'll call a cab."

The cab arrived within a few minutes and they set off. It was mid-summer, and at Edinburgh's latitude there would be light until at least eleven. Even now, the slanting sun was still shining on the tops of the trees and the slate roofs of the crescent that led to Bruntsfield. They passed a group of teenagers on their way to the tennis courts at the bottom of the road. They passed a woman cajoling a reluctant West Highland terrier on its evening walk. They saw a man washing a car with a bucket of soapy water, his expression one of distaste at the task he was being obliged to perform.

"That's a very dirty car, that one," said Jamie. "I walked past it the other day. It was covered in dust and bird droppings."

"I need to wash my car," said Isabel. "I haven't washed it for . . . oh goodness, a year . . . or two."

Jamie suddenly leaned over and kissed her. "You have better things to do," he whispered. "I'll wash your car. I promise you."

THE CASA TRIMALCHIO was in St. Mary Street, in the Old Town, a few doors down from the World's End pub. It was an area of cobbled streets and old tenements, not far from the Palace of Holyroodhouse and the Scottish Parliament. Because of its position, it was popular with politicians, and the civil servants who advised them. It was also used by journalists covering the Parliament or working in the BBC studios not far away. It was not a place for a quiet dinner for those who didn't want to be seen, although the proprietor, Lucca Bompiani, had a way of keeping political opponents from being seated in close proximity to one another. He also had a rule, enforced firmly but tactfully, to the effect that those who wished to discuss politics should do so in a way that could not be heard at any neighbouring table.

The restaurant was not busy when Isabel and Jamie arrived, and they were shown to their table straightaway. They looked at the menu, an elaborate, hand-written list of Italian specialities. Jamie looked at the wine list, muttering about the prices.

"Don't," said Isabel. "You told me not to worry. You yourself said that. You told me not to worry about money."

Jamie pointed to one of the wines on the list. Leaning forward, he explained his objection in a low voice. "I know for a fact what that costs in the supermarket. They have that exact wine—same vintage, the lot—in Morningside. It's eleven pounds there. Eleven. And here? Fifty-six."

"It's always more expensive in a restaurant," said Isabel. "That's a fact of life. They have to make a profit."

"But that's a mark-up of over four hundred per cent," said Jamie. "More, perhaps, given that they won't have paid eleven pounds for it. More like seven, or even six."

"They have to pay their waiters," said Isabel. "But let's not quibble, Jamie."

Jamie lowered the wine list. "Sorry, you're right. Let's look at the menu itself."

The waiter appeared, notebook in hand, ready to take their order. He reeled off a list of specials that were not on the printed menu.

Isabel asked about the monkfish and Jamie enquired about the Tuscan bean stew.

"It's very simple," the waiter replied. "I wouldn't recommend it. Beans are, well, beans. Of course, if that's what you like . . ."

They settled on a plate of antipasti each, to be followed by monkfish. Wine was ordered too, and a bottle of mineral water. Isabel looked across the table at Jamie. She reached out to take his hand.

"This is so nice," she said. "If this is what you like."

He glanced at the retreating figure of the waiter. "Very odd," he said. "Waiters aren't meant to warn you off things."

"He said a very Edinburgh thing," said Isabel. "Remember the wonderful line from Jean Brodie? **For those who like that sort of thing, that is the sort of thing they like.** Bone-deep disapproval disguised as tolerance."

"But Edinburgh's only **slightly** disapproving," said Jamie. "And anyway, it's loosened up."

A new group of diners entered the restaurant—two men and two women. They were somewhere in their early forties and smartly dressed. The men both wore suits, although one was sporting an open-necked shirt; the other man had a striped tie. One of the women was in a black trouser suit, while the other had a green Indian print dress with what looked like a silk shawl. The woman in the trouser suit had a double string of pearls around her neck. One of the men had large horn-rimmed spectacles of the sort that might be described as a fashion statement.

As the new arrivals were shown to their table by Lucca himself, Jamie whispered to Isabel, "See him? The one in the specs? See him?"

Isabel glanced across the restaurant. The man had looked vaguely familiar to her, but she had not been able to place him. "That's . . ." She shook her head. "Who is he?"

"He's called Hugh Maclean," said Jamie. "You see him on television. He has a column in the paper, and he runs that think tank— you know, the one that comes up with those predictions. The one that tells everybody else that they're doing everything wrong."

"Which they often are," said Isabel. "We ignore think tanks at our peril."

Jamie smiled. "It's an odd expression, isn't

it? What do you imagine when somebody says **think tank**? Do you see them all sitting about in a tank of some sort—perhaps half submerged—thinking about things?"

Isabel was enjoying this. "Not quite, but that's a nice image. I think more of . . . well, I suppose I think of an ivory tower. A tall, ivory-coloured building with a room at the top, which is the think tank."

Jamie leaned forward. "And then every so often somebody emerges—some rather wild-looking type with untidy hair and professorial glasses—and announces what the think tank has thought. And it's duly noted down, and then they move on to thinking about the next thing they have to think about." He paused, and then, looking across the restaurant again, he added, "And that woman. The one with the pearls . . ."

Isabel followed his gaze. "The pearls are on the wrong woman. The one in the dress should be wearing them."

"Possibly," said Jamie. "But that's not what I was going to say. I recognise her."

Isabel asked him who she was.

"She's a member of the Scottish Parliament.

She's in the Lib Dems, I think. She had a big run-in with the Catholic Church over that guardianship business. She and the Catholic archbishop had a spectacular bust-up on television. A real **stushie**." Jamie used the Scots word to describe a brawl; like many Scots words, it was highly suggestive. A **stramash** in Scots was a chaotic argument or mix-up; a **stushie** was something that, although possibly verbal, could also involve an exchange of blows.

Isabel recalled the debate. "I think I remember her now. She doesn't mince her words."

"No," said Jamie. "She sautés them and they come out pretty hot."

An antipasti trolley arrived at their table, and they busied themselves with making their selections. The waiter who had warned against the bean stew now expressed reservations about the asparagus. "It's not in its first flush of youth," he said. "The artichokes are nice, though. And this salami here, this one, is seriously good. I'd eat it myself."

They made their choices, and the waiter wheeled the trolley away.

"Curiouser and curiouser," said Isabel. "Do you think he likes his job?"

"Probably not," said Jamie.

The waiter was now talking to the political table. And at this point the door opened, and another party of diners arrived. This was a smaller group of just two men—one a man in his mid-fifties, slightly corpulent and with that sleek, well-groomed look of the financier; the other an earnest-looking younger man in a sharply tailored chalk-stripe suit.

Jamie's interest was immediately aroused. He reached across the table and tapped Isabel's wrist.

"Central casting's being kind to us," he whispered. "Everybody's here, it seems."

Isabel followed his gaze across the room. "I'm hopelessly out of touch," she said. "I don't know who anybody is."

"Don't stare," said Jamie.

"I'm not," she protested. "You're the one who's staring."

Jamie put a finger to his lips. The two newcomers were waiting to be seated and were looking about the restaurant.

"They can't hear us," said Isabel. "There's too much noise from Hugh Maclean's table."

Jamie spoke above a whisper, but still in subdued tones. "That's Mark Throsby, the asset-stripper."

Isabel shot another glance across the restaurant. "The man who—"

"Yes," interjected Jamie. "The man who bought Macdonald Shipbuilding. And then threw it to the wolves—although he, actually, was the main wolf, as it turned out."

"Remind me," said Isabel. "I saw it in the papers, but I didn't really follow it."

Jamie took a bite of artichoke. "He bought Macdonald. He promised the workforce that everything would be all right. He accepted a big government grant to keep the yard going. Then he split the company up and sold its assets, including its own shipyard, which he sold to a property development company—owned by himself—and turned into expensive flats with a view of the Clyde." He paused, glancing in Throsby's direction. "Something like four hundred men lost their jobs."

Isabel looked down at her plate. That was the problem, she thought; that was why she felt uncomfortable about that fund of hers, managed for her by investment advisers who swore blind they would invest only in ethical companies. But how did one know who was ethical and who was not? The whole system seemed to be infected, top to bottom, with the suppurating corruption of greed.

Lucca now detached himself from Hugh Maclean and made his way over to Throsby and his companion. He shook hands with them and then invited them to follow him to the table next to the Maclean table.

Jamie watched. "He's putting them right next to his sworn enemies," he said under his breath. "Hugh Maclean spent a lot of time on television denouncing Throsby and all his works."

They watched as the two newcomers sat down. They did not appear to have noticed their nearby company, but Hugh Maclean had. He stared intensely at them, and then turned to his fellow diners and said something to them. They turned and looked in the direction of Throsby's table. One of them, the woman in the Indian print dress, threw up her hands in a gesture of undisguised horror.

What happened next took place quickly. As if conducted by an unseen hand, all of Hugh Maclean's party rose to their feet, pushing their chairs back noisily. Then, their table napkins discarded on the table and the floor, they pointedly walked out. Hugh Maclean shouted something to Lucca, who seemed to be paralysed. The waiter, looking confused, opened the door for them to depart.

There were four other tables occupied at the time. All of those seated at these tables saw what happened, and were reduced to silence. Lucca dithered for a few moments, and then strode over to Throsby and whispered something in his ear, patting him on the shoulder as he did so. Throsby nodded, and then, turning to his dining companion, shrugged.

Lucca clapped his hands to signal to the waiters to attend to the diners. Isabel and Jamie's waiter came to their table and grinned at them. "Our very first walk-out," he said. He lowered his voice. "Not that I blame them."

"He's not a popular man," Jamie said.

The waiter cast a glance in the direction of the two shunned diners. "That," he said, "is probably his only friend." He smiled wickedly.

"You know all those stories about waiters spitting in the soup behind the scenes? You've heard those? Well, everything they say is true. We **do,** but only in the case of those who **really** deserve it."

Jamie smiled.

"I can understand the temptation," Isabel muttered. "But—"

The waiter did not give her the time to finish her qualification. "Yes," he said, "it's very tempting, I can tell you. I won't do it this time because . . . well, they haven't ordered soup. Wise, perhaps. They might know the danger—people like that could know, I think. You go and mess up people's lives and you think: Are they going to spit in my soup now? And the answer you might just come up with is **yes.**"

He threw a final glance over towards Throsby, and then professionalism reasserted itself. Changing the subject, he pointed to their plates. "Everything okay? Wise move not to have the asparagus, by the way."

Jamie nodded, and the waiter returned to the kitchen. Isabel sat back in her chair. She was thinking.

"Are you all right?" asked Jamie.

Isabel gave a cursory nod. "Yes, I'm fine. But I can't say I approve of what we've just seen."

"It was hardly surprising," said Jamie. "And frankly, that man deserves everything he gets."

Isabel ignored this. "Do you know, I'm doing a special issue of the **Review** on the ethics of food. I've got Julian to do a major piece for me." Julian was Julian Bagnini, a friend of Isabel's, who had written on the subject of food and its ethics.

"And we have an article on commensality lined up," Isabel continued. "It's about the moral bond between those who eat together. But it also deals with the issue of when you can refuse to eat with somebody."

"Whenever you want, surely," said Jamie. "I don't have to have breakfast with somebody I don't like."

"In the privacy of your own home," said Isabel. "You can choose your company there. But you can't choose it in public places—like restaurants."

"Why not?"

"Because everyone is entitled to eat in public eating places."

Jamie was looking over to the Throsby table. "Even people like that?"

Isabel inclined her head. "Even people like that."

Jamie thought about this. Isabel was right, he felt: you had no right to require your fellow diners to be acceptable to you. And yet Isabel's position was susceptible to counter-arguments. He immediately thought of an extreme case: What if you found yourself in a restaurant full of members of the Ku Klux Klan enjoying an annual dinner? Would you feel obliged to stay and finish your meal? He did not think he would, and nor, he imagined, would Isabel.

He was thinking about this when Isabel suddenly stood up. He looked up at her. Was she going to walk out too, even after what she had just said? "You aren't going to—"

She cut him short with a shake of her head. "I'll be back in a moment."

He watched as she crossed the room to the table where Throsby and the young man were seated. Because of the peculiar acoustic of the room, he heard every word of what was said.

"Mr. Throsby," Isabel began. "I'm sorry that you were subjected to that. It was discourteous. It was wrong."

It took Throsby a few moments to react. Then, he rose to his feet, inclining his head as he did so. "Thank you. I . . . I . . ." He spread his hands in a gesture that signified that he was at a loss for words.

"I'm not saying that I sympathise with what you do—your financial dealings, shall I say—but I do not think you deserve to be publicly shunned like that."

Again, Throsby inclined his head. "It's very good of you. Thank you. I appreciate your gesture—I really do."

Isabel nodded and turned on her heels to get back to her table. At neighbouring tables there was complete silence: everyone in the restaurant had followed the exchange. At one table in particular, an elderly man, seated in a party of four, watched open-mouthed. He stared at Isabel. A few minutes later, he called Lucca over and whispered something to him. Lucca replied. Isabel and Jamie saw none of this.

Jamie said to Isabel, "I'm really rather proud of you, you know."

She smiled. "I'm proud of you too."

Jamie took a sip of wine. "I would never have done that. It wouldn't have occurred to me. I'm not that brave."

"Really?" said Isabel. "I think you are, you know. I think you're as brave as William Wallace himself."

Jamie laughed. "Braveheart? I don't think so." He paused. "But it's good of you to say that. Nobody else ever has."

"Because the occasion has never arisen," said Isabel. "You never know how brave you're going to be—until the occasion arises."

"I'm not brave," Jamie insisted. "I could never have flown a Spitfire in the Battle of Britain."

Isabel disagreed. "You can't say that. And I suspect you would. I suspect you'd have been there, with the rest of them, doing what had to be done."

Jamie shook his head. "Some of them had only—what was it—twelve hours of training before they went up. Something like that."

"And they saved everything," said Isabel. "Europe. The world, perhaps. It was close, wasn't it?"

Jamie nodded. "It was."

Isabel realised that she had never asked Jamie about his views on pacifism: the subject had never come up. And yet it was something very basic, a fundamental question—and you should know, shouldn't you, what your own husband thought about that? Now she asked him.

"You said you wouldn't have been brave enough to fly a Spitfire," she began, "but would you have flown it, if you had been a bit braver? Not that I think you wouldn't be brave enough, but . . ."

"Would I if I could?"

"Yes."

He hesitated, but not for long. "Of course."

She was relieved by the answer. "So, you'd fight for a just cause?"

He nodded. "Wouldn't you?" He looked at her. "If somebody came along and threatened Charlie and Magnus—you'd . . . you'd kill them if necessary? If there was no other way of saving them?"

She replied without thinking. "Yes. If there was no alternative. Yes, I'd do whatever needed to be done." She returned his gaze. "You'd do the same, wouldn't you?"

"Without a moment's hesitation."

She looked down at her hands. Hands were capable of that, and more. It was a hand that must have pulled the lever that released the bomb on Hiroshima. One human hand. But even that was not simple; had that hand not gone through that motion, then Japan might not have surrendered and there could have been millions more deaths in the invasion that followed. It was far from simple. There was a calculus of life and death with which politicians and generals had to wrestle, and whatever they did there were human costs.

"It's very complex," said Isabel, but then added, "That antipasti was delicious, wasn't it? It's made me . . ." She hesitated. Suddenly she felt strangely, overwhelmingly happy. She was with the man she loved more than she had loved anybody ever before, and he was **hers.** At that moment, nothing else mattered to her—nothing. Was this what love really was? she wondered—a feeling of pure delight in the object of one's love; the desire that the other person should just **be,** and that you, the smitten one, the faithful one, should in some indefinable way enhance that state of being.

That that's what was meant by the idea of loving another for himself alone.

Jamie was the man she loved, she told herself—this is the person whom I love, although I could easily, I suppose, have ended up loving somebody else, or even loving an idea, a place, even something distant and unattainable. What was it that Auden said? Love requires an object—**anything will do.** Then he went on to say, **When I was a child I loved a pumping engine, thought it every bit as beautiful as you . . .**

Those were beautiful lines, she thought, and they emphasised, quite rightly, what one might call the **accident** of love. There was a lot of chance in love—a lot of luck—but there was not too much point in thinking about that, other than to thank whatever gods one believed in, or blind fate if one believed in none, for the way things had worked out. And for her, they had worked out as well as she could possibly have hoped for.

"What about the antipasti?" asked Jamie. "It's made you what?"

"Happy," said Isabel. "Just happy. You and the antipasti, that is, have made me happy."

CHAPTER TWO

GRACE STAYED OVERNIGHT, as she often did when babysitting. That suited Isabel and Jamie, as the boys, waking up to Grace's presence in the house, shot excitedly into her room, bounced on her bed with all the exuberance that only small boys can muster and insisted on a story. Parents, in such circumstances, were of no real interest, and this gave Isabel and Jamie a leisurely start to the day, further assisted by the fact that Grace, rather than Jamie, would be taking Charlie to school. Jamie was teaching that day, which meant that he would spend the entire day, from ten onwards, at the Edinburgh Academy, on the opposite side of the city. That day he had the worst of his students. "Mark Brogan," Jamie announced, with a groan. "That boy destroys every piece he tries to play. He has no sense of timing at all—none. He just can't count."

Isabel smiled. She had met Mark's parents at an Academy concert, and they had expressed pride in their son's performance. "And just think," remarked Mrs. Brogan, a woman with a hairstyle of tight blonde curls, "here are Jim and I with absolutely no musical talent between us, not a scrap, and there's Mark getting on by leaps and bounds."

Mark's father had expressed a similar view, but had gone further. He wondered why it was that their son had not been offered a place in the school orchestra. Could Jamie do anything about that? Not that they were asking for any favours—"We wouldn't want to put you in a spot"—but that Macleod boy, the one who played the trumpet, was not very good at all and he, somehow or other, had been accepted into the orchestra. Did Isabel not think that was odd, especially given that Mark, who practised so hard, was denied a place?

Isabel had replied, as gently as she could, that she really had nothing to do with the school orchestra, and that Jamie, although he was a member of the Academy's music staff, was only a part-time tutor. "I don't think he has anything to do with who gets picked for the orchestra," she said. "If he did, he might be able to do something, but I don't think it works that way."

Mrs. Brogan had smiled sweetly. "Of course, of course. But sometimes a word in the right quarter—you know what I mean—might just help. We're the last ones to be pushy parents—the very last ones, I assure you . . ."

This had brought a nod of agreement from Mr. Brogan, who said, "Absolutely. Absolutely the last."

This conversation had occurred during the school concert interval, and Isabel had been relieved at this stage by the sounding of a bell; the second half of the concert was about to begin. "Oh well," she said, "I'm sure that Mark will make progress. Jamie says that he works hard at his bassoon." She gestured to the drift of parents making their way back to their seats. "I suppose we'd better be getting back in."

Mrs. Brogan seemed satisfied with the

exchange. "It's so kind of you to take it up," she said. "Sometimes schools are a bit—how shall I put it?—a bit impersonal when it comes to these things. Talented children, like Mark, can get left behind."

This had alarmed Isabel, who was punctilious when it came to moral obligation. It would not do for somebody to believe that she had agreed to do something that in reality she had not agreed to do. She would need to spell it out again.

"I don't think Jamie can do anything about the orchestra, Mrs. Brogan. I really don't."

But Mrs. Brogan appeared not to hear this; she had broken off to have a word with another mother whom she had recognised in the crowd.

And now, as Jamie prepared to leave the kitchen, his mention of Mark Brogan reminded her that she had not told him about this conversation at the concert.

"That boy," she said, frowning. "I forgot to tell you about his mother."

Jamie groaned. **"La Brosse?"** he said. "That's what the piano teacher calls her. The Brush. Her hair—those curls . . ."

Isabel suppressed a smile. Jamie was naturally kind—and tactful—but he seemed to delight in nicknames. He never invented these himself, but he was not averse to using ones created by others. **La Brosse** was perhaps a bit uncharitable—and Jamie was certainly not that by nature. Isabel wondered whether she should point out to him—gently, of course—that one could not help curly hair, and it would presumably be hurtful to Mrs. Brogan if she heard that her son's music teacher called her the Brush. But she did not. She never lectured him, even if he occasionally told her what he thought one should do, or, more often, what one should **not** do, namely, **not** interfere in the lives of others, even if they asked you to do exactly that. So now, of Mrs. Brogan and her curly hair—which **did** look rather like a brush—she simply said, "Yes, her."

"Her hair," said Jamie. "Do you think she puts it in curlers? Or is it natural?"

Isabel had no idea. "Some people have naturally curly hair, I suppose. She might be one."

"It's amazing," Jamie mused. "Imagine looking like that."

Isabel frowned. Yes, imagine looking like

another person. Perhaps that was what we should do more often. **Put yourself in their shoes** was a familiar piece of advice, but it might be particularised into **Imagine looking like her.** That brought it home, because that was often the issue with how the world treated people. If you stood out, you were vulnerable. If you were excessively overweight, or very small, or if you walked in an odd way, then people treated you differently from the way they treated those who were none of those things. They might not do that so readily if they could imagine what it was to be you. And although there was no reason why the way you looked should be **you,** that was the way in which the world tended to see things. The way you looked could be taken as **you,** whatever was going on inside.

"Anyway, what about her?"

"She said something at that concert. She implied that I'd agreed to speak to you about getting her son into the orchestra."

Jamie snorted in astonishment. "The Foghorn?" he exclaimed. "Put the Foghorn in the school orchestra?"

Isabel sighed. "Is that what you call him?

Really, Jamie, nicknames are all very well, but aren't they a bit childish sometimes?"

Jamie smiled. "All right. No nicknames—although I didn't invent that one. That's what I heard one of the boys calling him. Obviously Mark's bassoon-playing reminded him of a foghorn. Quite accurate, I thought." He made a serious face. "But I won't call him that. I shall be completely professional—I promise you. So, young Mark Brogan . . . What am I meant to do?"

"She wanted you to get him into the orchestra. She wanted me to speak to you about it. I tried to tell her that it was nothing to do with you, but I don't think that sunk in. And then she went off to speak to somebody else, and I didn't have the chance to explain to her that there was nothing I could do."

Jamie sighed. "But now you have spoken to me. You've done what she asked you to do." He paused, and gave Isabel a stern look. "Isabel, I know that you're a philosopher. I know that you worry a lot about moral obligation. I know that. But you aren't responsible for **everything.**" His stern look became one of frustration. "You don't owe La

Brosse . . . I mean Mrs. Brogan, anything. Don't be ridiculous."

At one level, Isabel knew that he was right. She had given Mrs. Brogan no grounds for thinking that she could do anything to help her, and they were, in that respect, moral strangers. Or were they? You could owe a duty to people who imagined they had a claim on you—that could be the case if you knew that they were relying on you and you allowed that reliance to continue. She would have to make it clear to Mrs. Brogan, perhaps, that she should **not** think Isabel could do anything. Perhaps it would have to be spelled out.

For Jamie, the matter was settled. He looked at his watch. He would have to go if he were not to be late for Mark Brogan's lesson.

He moved round to Isabel's side of the table and kissed her cheek. "Don't worry about these things," he said. "Life's too short. I'll speak to her next time I see her. I'll tell her that there's zero chance of Mark getting into the orchestra."

"But she's so keen . . ."

Jamie sighed. "I'd like to get into the Berlin

Philharmonic," he said. "But it's not going to happen."

Isabel smiled. "Do you want me to have a word with the conductor's wife?"

This brought a laugh from Jamie. "Or his mother?"

The telephone rang. Jamie answered, and passed the receiver over to Isabel. It was Cat.

Isabel knew what was coming. When Cat phoned at breakfast time it was because there was a staffing issue at her delicatessen in Bruntsfield. Eddie would have slept in, or the woman who helped on Fridays had had to go off to Aberdeen to visit her sick mother, or something of that sort. And Isabel would inevitably reply that she would be only too happy to help and would be there within the hour, and Cat would say, "I really don't know what I would do without you," and Isabel would reply, "I don't mind, you know. I really don't mind." On this occasion, it was Cat who had to be out of the shop between ten and lunchtime. Eddie would be there, she explained, but they were likely to be busy and would need two people.

The telephone call over, as he left the room Jamie said, "The usual?"

"Yes," said Isabel. "But Grace is here and she's going to be taking the boys to nursery and to school. I did have some editing to do, but . . ."

"Which you won't be able to do?"

"Evidently not."

Jamie hesitated. "She takes advantage of you, you know."

Isabel made a gesture of acceptance. "Family."

"Yes," said Jamie. "But she could offer to pay you, don't you think? And she should also bear in mind that you have a life to lead."

Isabel knew the arguments. It was probably true that Cat was rather too ready to call on her for help, but she had a business to run, and if there was nobody else to assist, then Isabel was happy enough to step in. And she enjoyed working in the delicatessen, even if it could be exhausting. Slicing Parma ham and ladling stuffed olives into small cardboard containers was very different from running the **Review of Applied Ethics,** but therein, she thought, lay the charm of such pursuits. If you had no philosophical review to edit, then perhaps the shine would go off ham and olives; but if you did, then the world of the delicatessen could seem exotic.

"Don't worry about me," she said to Jamie. "I know how to handle Cat." Even as she spoke, she wondered whether that was, in fact, the case. The truth of the matter was that she handled Cat with kid gloves, tiptoeing round issues that she knew to be sensitive. She rarely turned down any request from Cat, nor criticised her for what she did. Even when Cat chose to involve herself with unsuitable men—and that had very much been the pattern of her niece's emotional life—Isabel was careful about expressing a view. Cat, she believed, did not want to hear what Isabel thought about the men in her life, and so it was best not to say anything. None of that, she thought, amounted to knowing how to handle Cat.

Jamie cast his eyes upwards. He, too, thought Cat difficult. He had been in love with Isabel's niece once—a long time ago—and he was pleased that was no longer the case. "Just don't let her browbeat you," he said. "Help her today, but tell her that she will need to get somebody else tomorrow. You can't give her all your time—you have your own job to do, your own life to lead." He hesitated at the door, as if uncertain about whether to say more. But he had to go: Mark Brogan would be waiting for him.

Isabel blew him a kiss, but did not say anything. The kiss said, **You're right,** and he was, but he was not the one who had to deal with Cat. She did—and it was never as easy as it sounded in theory, particularly when it came to working out where to start. And that, perhaps, was why so many difficult people got away with it: other people simply did not know where to start.

SHE WALKED SLOWLY along Merchiston Crescent, stopping twice on the way—once to acknowledge a cat that appeared from a gateway, looked up at her and meowed a vocal greeting that quickly turned into a purr. The cat rubbed himself briefly against Isabel's legs, uttered a further meow and then returned to its garden. The second stop was to help a woman who had dropped her shopping bag on her pavement. It had contained, amongst other things, eggs that were now broken. Yolk dripped out of the bag and onto the ground. "They're organic," said the woman. "The yolks of some of the eggs you get in the supermarket these days are dreadfully pale." The woman's newspaper, a copy of that morning's **Scotsman,** was damp with egg white. The photograph of a well-known politician stared out from the front page. "He's left with egg on his face," said the woman, as she thanked Isabel for retrieving a couple of lemons that had rolled into the road.

Arriving at the delicatessen, Isabel was greeted by Cat's assistant, Eddie, who was serving a customer, filling a small tub with marinated artichoke hearts.

"I could eat these all day," Eddie was saying to the woman before the counter.

"Me too," said the woman. "These, and green olives stuffed with garlic. Heaven."

Eddie glanced at Isabel and smiled. "Hi," he said. "She's still back there." He gave a toss of the head in the direction of Cat's office.

Isabel acknowledged the greeting, nodded to the woman and made her way into the office at the back of the store. There she found Cat at her desk, staring at a page of figures. She looked up and smiled as Isabel entered the room. "Can you understand this?" she asked, handing Isabel the piece of paper.

Isabel looked at the printed heading: **Porter and Daughter: Wholesale Cheese Merchants.**

"What a lovely title. A refreshing change from **and Sons.** There are so many **and Sons** in business; one wondered when the daughters would get a look-in."

Cat shrugged. "I've never met Mr. Porter. He does exist, though. I've spoken to him on the phone. They're over in Glasgow. He has a very broad Glasgow accent."

"You don't normally associate that with cheese, do you?" Isabel looked up from the columns of figures on the paper. She could not make head nor tail of them. **Your order(s) Feb to June: Mull Traditional Farmhouse Cheddar 18 (6.9)?** And **Blue cheese (unspecified 43, 22, 11)?** "I'd imagine a cheese merchant speaking with a French accent. With lots of creamy vowels, as in Camembert." She thought of the daughter. What would it be like to be the daughter of Mr. Porter, cheese merchant? Had she always wanted to go into the business? Or had she yearned for something quite different—perhaps to be a doctor or a drama teacher or . . .

"Can you picture her?" asked Isabel.

"Picture her? Who?"

"Mr. Porter's daughter," said Isabel, handing the sheet of paper back to her niece. "I was wondering what she'd be like. Fair hair done in plaits? Quite well built—to be able to carry the cheese around? A blue gingham blouse?"

Cat ignored this. She was used to Isabel's tendency to go off at a tangent. "But can you understand what they mean? I can't. Is it weight they're talking about, or number of pieces? Or the age of the cheese? Six months? Nine months?"

"You could phone Mr. Porter . . . or his daughter . . ." Isabel wondered whether Mr. Porter's daughter liked being thought of as Porter's daughter. She would have a name, an identity of her own, and might resent people thinking of her as **the daughter.** And yet Mr. Porter would be proud of her: the title of the firm made that clear. He would be proud that his own daughter would be taking over the business in due course; proud that the name of Porter would continue to be associated with cheese. That was how the people who created these small businesses viewed the world, and understandably so.

Cat put the piece of paper aside. The Porters could wait. If they chose to be so obscure in their invoicing, then they should not be surprised if people were slow to pay. She looked up at Isabel. "Thanks for coming, by the way. I know it wasn't much notice."

Isabel had been wearing a scarf. She now hung this on a peg on the back of Cat's door and took one of the two freshly laundered striped aprons from a neighbouring peg.

"That's all right. I wasn't doing much." She thought: Just editing the **Review of Applied Ethics.** That's all.

"I'll be back by lunch," said Cat. "Or maybe just after . . . if you didn't mind doing lunchtime too."

"That's fine," said Isabel. Grace would be only too pleased to look after the boys after she fetched Charlie from school. There was a pile of clothing in the laundry that needed ironing, and Grace always liked to find an excuse not to tackle that. In Isabel's study there was a pile of books ready to be sent out for review, with covering letters still unwritten, her equivalent of un-ironed laundry. They could wait too.

Cat looked at her watch. "I'm going to have to head off in about ten minutes." She paused. "Can I ask you something?"

"Of course."

Cat hesitated before continuing. "You know the trust?"

Isabel nodded. This would be a financial request. The trust to which Cat was referring was the one set up by Isabel's maternal great-aunts from Alabama, from that ante-bellum house in Mobile that featured in all the old family photographs. The trust was funded, ultimately, by the Louisiana land and title company that had been in the family for some time, but its investments were now much more diverse, and were in twelve or more countries. Isabel was not sure how ethical they were: she encouraged her fellow trustees to be sensitive, to look at the social responsibility profile of the companies they financed, but she suspected that such credentials as they had in this respect went little further than window-dressing.

The precise origin of the funds themselves was obscure, but it was this money that funded Isabel—the principal beneficiary—and, to a much lesser extent, Cat. Under the terms of the trust, Cat was entitled to discretionary payments of such a level as to complement "within reasonable boundaries" her principal income, which, as the trust deed stated, "should be derived from her own endeavours." Isabel was a trustee, along with two Edinburgh lawyers, originally appointed by her father, who wore identical spectacles that made it difficult for her to distinguish between them: one was called MacGregor and the other was called MacGeorge, which made mistakes as to identity even more likely. In previous years the trust had helped Cat to purchase the delicatessen, to carry out various repairs to the premises, and to attend courses in food hygiene, culinary matters and business management. Some of these courses were in exotic places, and for this reason expensive, but the bills had been cheerfully footed for a ten-day

course on **charcuterie** in Tuscany, a week-
long wine sampling course in Bordeaux, and
a private tour of the olive estates of Campania
and Puglia.

Isabel waited for Cat to continue.

"Have you seen those two dusty characters recently? Hamish MacGregor and the
other one?"

Isabel corrected her. "Actually, it's Hamish
MacGeorge and Gordon MacGregor."

"I find it hard to tell the difference."

Isabel laughed. "So do I—they're rather like
Dupond and Dupont in the **Tintin** books.
Anglice, Thomson and Thompson."

Cat looked puzzled. **"Anglice?"**

Isabel was abashed. She realised she had
used a word of medieval Latin origin to talk
of the translation of French into English.
Bluestocking, she thought. Bluestocking. And
then she thought: No, the whole idea of blue-
stockings was insulting, and implied that
women should not have intellectual interests. She objected to that, but, now that she
thought about it, she was not so sure that Cat
would feel the same. On such occasions that
Cat had discussed Isabel's work with her, her

niece had wrinkled her nose at the mention of philosophy. And when she mentioned the word **philosophy**, Cat made a visual set of quotation marks with her fingers—a gesture that Isabel was wary of, especially when used like that. One might as well put quotation marks around **salami** or **olives.** Philosophy was every bit as real as these things. But this was not the time. "Sorry," she said. "In English. The English version of **Tintin** renames them."

Cat waited. "And?"

"And, yes, we had a meeting about three months ago. It was to look at the state of the markets. It went on rather long, I'm afraid, and my tummy started to rumble. It's very embarrassing, you know, when MacGeorge and MacGregor are going on about exposure to Greek government bonds and your stomach starts to growl."

Cat looked interested. "Do we . . . I mean the trust—have any Greek bonds?"

Isabel said that she had been told that they did, and that Greek bonds could pay off rather well, provided you had nerves of steel and were prepared to take a seventy-five per cent risk of default.

Cat was bemused. "That fusty twosome? They're secret risk-takers?"

"So it would seem. The trust deed actually authorises them to buy bonds issued by any government. That's what it says. When it was written, I suppose nobody imagined that there would be governments as shaky as the Greek one. So they had a little flutter—and it paid off. Five-year bonds, apparently, and they yielded . . . oh, I can't remember—eighty per cent in total? Something that impressive." She paused. "Why do you ask?"

Cat looked away. "I was just wondering." There was a note of hesitation in her voice. "I was just wondering: If I wanted to apply for something for the business—would there be funds?"

Isabel reassured her. "Of course there would be. That's one of the reasons it exists."

Cat said, "Yes, that. And also to keep you and Jamie in the style in which . . ." She stopped herself. Isabel was looking at her with dismay.

"I'm sorry," said Cat. "I didn't mean that."

Isabel brushed the remark aside, but she knew that they had strayed into an area that was fraught with difficulty. Jealousy. Isabel had all the money, and . . . and she had Jamie. Jamie used to belong to Cat, but now did not. Isabel had the money—and the man. One had to understand jealousy: there were some circumstances in which it would be surprising if it did **not** raise its head. "Write to Hamish MacGregor. Tell him what you need and what it's for."

"Gordon MacGregor, you mean."

"Yes. Him." Isabel frowned. "Or the other one. Hamish MacGeorge, or whatever. I don't think it matters. They work in the same firm. I'm sure they read each other's mail."

For a few moments, Isabel allowed her mind to wander. She imagined MacGregor and MacGeorge playing golf together and then having tea in the clubhouse, sharing a Dundee cake, allocating each piece with scrupulous fairness, as befitted the trustees of a family trust. She saw them sitting at a shared desk, counting Greek government bonds, a Greek dictionary at their side. She saw them doing a Zorba-type dance on the beach of a Greek island, still wearing their identical glasses, the sun on their pallid Scottish skin, with, in the background, a chorus of local fishermen and their wives clapping their hands in time to the music.

Cat was staring at her. "What are you thinking of, Isabel? You were somewhere else."

Isabel brought herself back to reality. "I was thinking of MacGregor and MacGeorge, as it happens."

Cat crossed the room. She glanced in the mirror that she kept on the wall, near the filing cabinet.

"Where are you off to?" asked Isabel.

Cat clearly did not want to answer. "I'm going into town," she replied. "George Street." The detail was given reluctantly, in a tone that indicated that Cat felt Isabel had no business asking.

Isabel reflected for a moment on Cat's lack of grace. There was a quality we called grace; we all knew that it existed—there were people we described as **gracious,** but we rarely thought about what was required for somebody to deserve that description. Courtesy came into it, but there was more to it than that. A person might be polite, might treat another with consideration, but still fail to show grace. Was it an attitude, then, of wanting others to feel good about themselves? Was it simple kindness, or was it kindness allied with a concomitant denial of self? To act graciously was to say: This is what you want, and I want you to have it for that reason. It was to do something you might not want to do, but to do it in a way in which others would never know about your reservations. Whatever it was, not explaining where she was going demonstrated a lack of grace on Cat's part. And that, thought Isabel, should be no surprise. Cat was not gracious. And yet, she went on to think, she is my niece, and whatever I might feel about her lack of grace, she is one for whom I **must** care.

"I was just asking," Isabel said mildly. "I was just asking because you asked me to come and relieve you and I . . ." She gave Cat a look that said, **Come on, can't you see?**

It did not work. Cat was ready to leave now, and she gave Isabel no reply. Instead, she said, "There's a whole new Spanish ham in the storeroom if you need it. It might be an idea to bring it through before the lunchtime rush."

Isabel nodded. "All right. I'll have a look."

"It needs tidying up," said Cat as she reached the door. "There's a layer of fat on part of it. I saw it. Eddie knows how to deal with it."

And with that, she left.

Isabel thought: Jamie was right; Cat takes advantage of me, and you shouldn't let people take advantage of you. You stood up to them. You said, "No, I can't come and help you in your deli because I want to get on with my own things and you never pay me anyway, and you need to think about the way you treat me . . ."

That advice, she told herself, was advice that should probably be widely offered. There were many who were in relationships in which a statement of that sort was long overdue. **Tread on me no longer.** That was what was needed to be said by the worm when it turned. She thought: **Henry VI, Part 3: To whom do lions cast their gentle looks? Not to the beast that would usurp their den. The smallest worm will turn being trodden on. And doves will peck in safeguard of their brood.**

She stopped herself. She was not in any

sense downtrodden. She helped Cat because she wanted to. Cat took it for granted, yes, but people did that, and being taken for granted was not, in itself, grounds for not doing what you freely undertook to do. The ungrateful took love for granted, but that did not mean that the love shown them should be withheld, or turned off, like a tap. And, anyway, you could not turn love off just like that. That was the whole point about love—it afflicted you; you had it in the same way as you had a cold. And you couldn't turn colds off; you sat them out, you waited until you recovered. It was the same with love.

CHAPTER THREE

ISABEL JOINED EDDIE behind the counter. The customer he had been serving had left, and there was nobody else. Eddie took a handkerchief out of his pocket and blew his nose loudly. Isabel looked at him.

"Eddie, are you going to wash your hands?"

He stared back at her. "I did. Earlier on."

Isabel tried to make light of it. "I know your nose is really clean . . ."

Eddie put his hands in the air. "No, you're right. Honest, I usually do, but sometimes, you know, you're not thinking, and . . . well, you know how it is."

She did. "I wasn't criticising you. I'm the

same. You stroke your chin and then you realise your hand has touched your lips and . . ."

"And then you've got spit on them," Eddie took up. "And you should see what's in spit. Boy, you should see. That food hygiene course I went on at Stevenson College—you remember I told you about it—they showed us slides on that course. They asked members of the course to spit on these slides, you see, and then they put them under this microscope and, ugh, there were all these bugs crawling about. Serious bugs."

Isabel smiled. "Not in **my** mouth," she muttered.

Eddie did not fully understand irony. He looked serious. "Even yours, Isabel. Not that I'm saying your mouth is more disgusting than anybody else's—it's probably just the same. Everybody has bugs. Everybody's crawling."

"What a delightful conversation, Eddie."

"You started it," he retorted. "You said my nose was full of bugs."

"Well, it is. I thought noses were famous for their fauna."

"It isn't fauna," Eddie objected. "It's microbiota. **Staphylococcus aureus.**"

She looked at Eddie with admiration. He appeared pleased. "I happen to know that. You didn't think I'd know, did you? But I even know the Latin name. That's what people have in their noses. You can get a really bad infection from that stuff—if it escapes from your nose, that is."

Isabel did not like the thought of a staphylococcal rampage. She pointed at the handkerchief in Eddie's hand. "I think you should wash your hands. All this talk of bugs, and the bugs are standing around laughing at us."

Eddie went to the small sink at the back of the room and washed his hands. Then he applied hand sanitiser before returning to the counter. "Satisfied?" he asked.

Isabel nodded. She raised the issue of the Spanish ham, and Eddie agreed that he would retrieve it from the storeroom later on. Isabel tidied up.

Customers came and went, keeping them busy until the mid-morning lull.

"You can have a coffee now," said Eddie. "I'll take ten minutes after you."

She prepared herself a latte and went to drink it, over a copy of that morning's

Scotsman, at one of the tables. She glanced at the headline: allegations of gross incompetence, lapping at the feet of a Scottish government minister, dominated the front page. Elsewhere in the paper, it was promised, there were revelations about the risk associated with intensive salmon farming. There was nothing good to report, it seemed.

Isabel sighed. She did not believe in burying her head in the sand, but there were times when she longed for a paper that portrayed the world in something other than a state of crisis. She wanted the world to be peaceful, and it was not. That was what lay behind talk of peace "the world cannot give." It cannot; much as we would like it to, it simply cannot. There were too many people—too many people arguing over scarce resources; too many people with differing ideas of what should be done with what we had; too many people who felt they had reasons to dislike others.

She lowered the paper, unsure whether she wanted to read about the government minister's embarrassment. He was probably not as inept as his enemies painted him. He would be doing his best, no doubt, and had made miscalculations, or not read something thoroughly enough, or simply forgotten what it was he was meant to do. Anybody could be in his position—even the braying pack of his opponents.

As she put the paper aside and took a first sip of her latte, she saw a man enter the deli and walk towards her table. She looked up, trying to place the vaguely familiar face. He was a man in his late sixties, she thought; a man of distinguished bearing, well dressed in a tweed jacket and a neatly knotted tie. The tie signified an institutional association—a medical school, or a medical college, perhaps—as woven into it there were slanted bands of tiny staffs of Asclepius. Men liked those tribal badges, she thought; women did not. Her eyes returned to his face, which was a Scottish face, she concluded, as the weather had made its mark. There were indoor faces and there were outdoor faces. This was the latter, she decided—the face of a rural doctor who liked hill-walking, some general practitioner from one of those small towns in the Borders, where there were long memories and obscure traditions. She tried again to remember where she had seen him. At a lecture at the museum or the Scottish National Gallery? At somebody's dinner party?

"Isabel Dalhousie?"

She nodded and smiled.

"Do you mind?" He gestured to the vacant chair on the other side of Isabel's table.

"Not at all," she said. "I'll have to get back to work in a few minutes, though—I'm staff, you see."

He lowered himself onto the chair. "I know that," he said. "But I also know that you're really a philosopher, not a . . . a delicatessen person."

"I'm a bit of both," said Isabel. She liked this man's voice—and his appearance too. He had one of those faces that if pressed to describe in one word one would say was distinguished. And his voice was what Grace would describe as **educated**—an embarrassingly old-fashioned way of describing a manner of speaking in which articulation was stressed and verbs, nouns and adjectives were used grammatically. But nobody used the term **educated voice** these days because it was redolent of elitism. Talk the way you want to, was today's message, and it doesn't matter if nobody can understand half of what you say, as long as the sounds you make are **authentic.**

She waited for him to pick up the social cues and introduce himself, which he did. "I'm Iain Melrose. We haven't actually met."

Melrose . . . She had been right about the Borders. The Border town of Melrose, about an hour outside Edinburgh, was exactly the sort of place for somebody like this, especially if he happened to be called Melrose. And that was not at all unusual: there were plenty of people whose ancestors had suffered from a lack of imagination in choosing their sur-names and had made a geographical choice. She had recently received a paper for publica-tion in the **Review** from a Professor Michel Paris, of the University of Paris, written with his co-author, Professor Valerie Lyon—of the University of Lyon. And now that she came to think of it, Jamie had recently spoken of a flautist in one of his ensembles, a Jenny Dublin, from Dublin.

"I thought we had," she said. "I thought I recognised you. We've seen one another, haven't we?"

He smiled, and she saw that he had a

small gold crown on one of his teeth. That was unusual, at least in Scotland. Having a gold tooth was a status symbol in some places; there were plenty of modern alternatives that could mimic a natural tooth—a gold tooth was jewellery. In Iain Melrose, she thought, this is wrong.

"We have indeed seen one another," he said. "Last night. I was having dinner . . ."

"Trimalchio's feast?"

He laughed at the reference. "The **Satyricon . . .** Did you see Fellini's take on that?"

"I did. A long time ago."

He looked wistful. "When films could still be works of art. Before pyrotechnics took over. Before the violence and the swearing."

She knew that he was right to express such regrets: good films, quiet and perceptive films, still existed but were largely drowned out by blockbusters made for an undiscriminating audience; and yet such observations, valid though they were, now sounded like a nostalgic yearning for something that had long since disappeared. Isabel could watch **Casablanca**

or Louis Malle time and time again, or
Pasolini, or Fellini, but Eddie, or Cat for that
matter, would watch none of these. Eddie
had once wandered unwittingly into a showing of classic Iranian films at the Filmhouse,
an art cinema on Lothian Road, and, being
unwilling to disturb an entire row of fellow
cinema-goers, had endured three hours of an-
guish. She had laughed at his descriptions, but
reminded herself that she had not had to sit
through a lengthy period of Iranian cinema
and might have felt a bit of what he felt.

She looked at Iain Melrose and felt a mo-
mentary unease. Was there something in this
encounter that she was misreading? He had
seen her at dinner and had somehow worked
out who she was, and had now turned up at
the deli. It suddenly crossed her mind that
he was trying to pick her up. But that, she
quickly decided, was highly unlikely. Men who
flirted with women they did not know did
not wear ties like that and were not called Iain
Melrose and—

"Please forgive the intrusion," he said.
"Somebody in the restaurant told me who

you were after you and your husband had left. I asked, you see, because I witnessed what happened."

Isabel sighed. "That display? That virtue-signalling performance by that table?"

Iain nodded. "Yes. It was appalling. I must confess I have no time for that particular man—not that I know him personally, but I followed that row over in Glasgow. One could hardly miss it."

"I didn't exactly approve either."

"I'm sure you didn't. But I suppose that sort of thing happens all the time. Irresponsible capitalism. Money doesn't stay in a hole, of course, but surely we can do better than that."

Isabel said that she thought we could. She saw that Eddie was looking at her from behind the counter. "I'm sorry," she said, "I'm going to have to get back to work shortly. My young colleague over there is giving me looks."

Iain took the hint. "I should come to the point. I witnessed the walk-out, but then I also saw what you did. I heard you too. I heard what you said to that man." He paused, and with a finger traced a pattern on the table-top—an invisible doodle. "I was tremendously impressed."

Isabel was not sure what to say. Compliments made her feel uncomfortable, as she felt that she did not really deserve them.

"I don't want to embarrass you," Iain continued. "But what you did was exactly the right thing to do. And I found myself thinking: **That's a brave person.**"

Isabel laughed. "It wasn't very much. I just felt a bit sorry for the man."

His expression was serious. "But it was the right thing, Isabel . . . if I may. It really was. Nobody cares about things these days. Nobody bothers to do the right thing. You did. You did it for all to see. You did the right thing."

"Well, you shouldn't shame another person like that. Not in those circumstances."

"I completely agree. And that was why I wanted to speak to you. I phoned up somebody who knows a bit about you . . ."

Her feeling of unease returned. Nobody likes to hear that somebody is calling others to make enquiries.

He might have sensed her unease. "I hope

you don't mind," he said hurriedly. "I'm not nosy, but I like to know who's who, and we do, in fact, have several mutual friends. The Gordons, for example. And Guy Peploe at the Scottish Gallery. I believe you know Guy."

She felt reassured. A person with a hidden agenda does not invoke shared acquaintanceship.

"I found out that you were often to be found working here," he continued, "and I came along on spec."

"May I ask why?"

He leaned forward to make his request. "Because I need to appoint an executor."

Isabel could not conceal her surprise. "Of your will? That sort of executor?"

He grinned—rather sheepishly, she thought. "Yes. Of my will."

Isabel was tempted to laugh. This was ridiculous: a perfect stranger—even if they did have friends in common—was asking her to agree to an office of trust.

"I'm flattered," she said. "But really, we don't know one another, and executors are usually people you know quite well. Or lawyers. They're not . . . well, people like me."

He brushed aside her objections. "I need somebody I can be sure is utterly upright. And who fits into that category these days?"

Isabel raised an eyebrow. "Lots of people, I'd have thought."

He looked at her askance. "Do you really think that? I think it's hard these days to find people who **care** about morality."

She replied that one had to be careful not to assume too readily that we lived in amoral times. Every generation, Isabel said, harboured that illusion.

He looked thoughtful. "Perhaps," he said. There was hesitation in his voice: he pointed out that there were good times and there were bad times—and the judgements as to where the boundaries were could be objectively justified. "The period between 1933 and 1945 was not a good time in Germany," he said. "And that's not a subjective judgement. Or Pol Pot's time in Cambodia. Or the Rwandan genocide. Or Japan after the invasion of Manchuria." He looked at her challengingly. "If you were Japanese in the 1930s, you might be forgiven for saying that you lived in amoral times."

Isabel was not so sure. "Such a person

might, of course, argue to the contrary. Ideas of morality and fanatical loyalty to the Emperor were all tied up with one another."

"But the Japanese still behaved immorally."

"I'm not sure one can condemn a whole people. The Japanese government was not the same thing as the Japanese people."

"But when a people tolerates crimes committed in its name?"

"Yes—the ones who allowed it, who did nothing, may have something to answer for. But it's not always easy for them." She paused. "If I had lived in Germany in 1940, I'm not sure that I would have the courage to resist tyranny. You could end up in a concentration camp."

He took time to consider this, and then he continued, "So what do you think of our own times?"

Isabel shrugged. "We're feeling our way."

Iain looked thoughtful. "And the state of the virtues?" he said. "Have you read Gertrude Himmelfarb, by any chance?"

"The American historian?"

"Yes. Her. She wrote about the loss of the virtues. How our moral focus has shifted."

Isabel knew the book. Eddie caught her eye once more. "I really have to get back to work," she said.

"I only read her recently," Iain said. "But what she said chimed with me. She feels we are focusing on some pretty small things in our moral debate and have lost sight of the virtues. We're obsessed with avoiding offence to others, but we spend absolutely no time on recommending the virtues." He paused. "I think she's right, you know."

It was a big subject, and Isabel once again could not help but glance at her watch.

He prepared to rise to his feet. "Yes, I'm imposing on you. I shouldn't keep you. But if you're wondering why I've approached you, it's because of what I saw you do. And then, everything people have told me about you backs up my judgement. I've heard that you really do weigh things up morally. A number of people have said that of you."

"I take an interest in moral questions," said Isabel. "That's what I do as a philosopher. But that doesn't make me some sort of paragon—an observer, perhaps, but not a paragon."

"Good enough for me," said Iain. "And may I just say this: Please don't reject my request out of hand."

There was a note in his voice that told Isabel this was a serious cry for help. And try as she might to play down any virtue on her part, she could never turn down a serious moral request emanating from within the circle of her moral concern. And this man, stranger though he might be, was within that circle: he was seated on the chair in front of her and that was, by any standards, within the sphere of her moral concern.

"All right," she said, rising from the table. "I have to get back to work, but you may come and see me about this, if you'd like to."

He looked relieved. "I shall. And it's good of you to offer."

They made arrangements. He would come to the house the following afternoon at three. She had a dental appointment at one-thirty, but she should be back in time. "I'll have to watch the time a bit," she said. "I have rather a lot of work on my plate at the moment. But half an hour or so should be fine."

"That," he said, "will be more than enough for something that demands only a binary response—yes or no."

Iain left, and Isabel returned to the counter. Eddie nodded towards the street. "What did he want?" he asked.

"He wants me to be the executor of his will," said Isabel. "He asked me out of the blue."

"You don't know him?"

Isabel shook her head. "No. We'd never met."

"Executor?" asked Eddie. "Is that the same as executioner?"

Isabel laughed. "No, not quite."

"It would be odd," said Eddie, "to ask somebody in your will to chop off another person's head."

"Odd," agreed Isabel. "And illegal."

"Nobody deserves to have their head chopped off," said Eddie.

Isabel was quick to agree. "I detest capital punishment," she said.

"So do I," said Eddie. "It's so unkind."

"Yes. It offends the principle of mercy." She reached for a pair of disposable gloves: she had to slice ham and then she would need to marinate more artichoke hearts, as they had almost run out.

"You know where Cat's gone?" Eddie remarked.

"Into town," said Isabel. "That's all she said to me."

"She told me it was George Street," said Eddie. "And I bet I know why she wanted to go down there."

Isabel waited for him to expand.

"There's Hamilton and Inches on George Street," Eddie said. "You know that grand jewellery place? That's where she went."

Isabel asked him why he thought that.

"Because she was going to be meeting Leo on George Street," Eddie said. "I heard her talking to him on the phone. She said, 'I'll meet you there.' Then she said, 'I hope it'll be ready.'"

"What would be ready?"

Eddie smirked. "The engagement ring."

Isabel drew in her breath. "How do you know that?"

"Because I can tell," said Eddie. "I can tell when chemistry's going really well. Cat's mad about Leo—I can tell you that, Isabel."

Isabel concentrated on slicing the Serrano ham. She picked up a fragment and popped it into her mouth. She knew that this was a bad idea, as the strong, salty taste would simply make her want more. That was the problem with anything salty: you craved more, and it took willpower to resist.

"May I have a piece?" asked Eddie.

Isabel cut a slice and skewered it before passing it to him.

Eddie took the offering and nibbled at it before putting the rest into his mouth. "I could live on ham," he said. "Just ham. Breakfast, lunch, dinner."

"You'd get scurvy," said Isabel. "That was why sailors had to suck on lemons. If they stuck to the salt beef available, then they'd be vitamin C–deficient."

Eddie nodded. "We're all deficient in vitamin D in Scotland. Did you know that, Isabel? We're so far north that we don't get enough sunlight."

Isabel said she took a supplement in the winter months.

A woman came into the delicatessen, followed by two girls in their late teens. The teenagers were showing one another something on their phones and sniggering. One of them looked at Eddie and whispered something to her friend, whose **sotto voce** reply set them off in giggles. Isabel sighed. If there was one stage of life through which one might be relieved to have passed, then the teenage years must be that stage.

Eddie blushed. "Stupid," he muttered.

Isabel reached out and touched his arm gently, in a gesture of solidarity. "Ignore them," she said under her breath.

"The tall one's called Rosie Mclaurin," said Eddie. "She lives near us in Craigmillar. She's already been pregnant. She has a job selling popcorn at the cinema."

"Oh, I see," Isabel said.

"She got pregnant in the cinema," Eddie continued. "It was in a **Star Wars** film."

The woman was now at the counter. She cast a disapproving glance at the girls, who moved off to examine something on the shelves. Isabel approached the woman. "Is there anything I can help you with?"

The woman consulted a scrap of paper on which she had pencilled a list. She wanted

smoked almonds, ninety per cent cocoa chocolate, and an Orcadian cheese that she had
previously bought there and that she wanted
to try again. "You had very little of it," she
said. "But it went down very well with my
husband. He's from the Orkneys, you see."

Isabel knew the cheese. Once again, they
had very little, but she could give the woman
what they had. "We have hardly any of this
cheese," she said, "because the woman who
makes it has only one cow."

This brought laughter.

"It's true," said Eddie. "I saw an article
about her in a magazine. She has one cow and
a whole flock of geese. She lives on Westray."

Isabel located the small package of cheese,
wrapped in greaseproof paper, and handed
it to the customer. "I'll find the smoked almonds," she said.

As she began to leave the counter, she felt
Eddie tug at her sleeve.

"Over there," he said, nodding in the direction of the two young women. "Rosie's
nicking something."

Isabel looked up sharply. The two young
women were standing in front of a display of

expensive Belgian chocolate bars. Isabel saw a quick movement of the hand as another chocolate bar was slipped into a canvas tote bag.

"I'll deal with this," she said to Eddie.

The woman to whom she had given the cheese had seen what was happening. "Wee thieves," she said. She did not lower her voice, and Rosie Mclaurin spun round.

"Youse calling us what?" she shouted.

They turned away, flustered. Isabel approached the young women.

"Don't you call us thieves," spat out Rosie. And then, to Eddie, "You been talking about us, Eddie? You spreading lies again, you wee minger?"

"I think you may have inadvertently slipped something into your bag," said Isabel. "Give it to me and I'll ring it up."

"Don't you accuse me," spat Rosie. "Heather, come with me—we don't have to stand here and hear all this . . ."

She did not finish. Cat came through the door, accompanied by Leo. She was smiling broadly. Sensing that she was outnumbered, Rosie and her friend walked quickly towards the door. Cat, not realising what was going on, held it open for them.

"She's stealing!" Eddie shouted out. But it was too late—the two young women had disappeared out onto the street.

Isabel shrugged. "I did my best," she said. And then, to Cat, she said, "You're early. I wasn't expecting you until after lunch."

Cat held out her left hand. "Engaged," she said.

Isabel took a deep breath. She had to smile, and she did so. "Well," she enthused, "congratulations, both of you." She paused. "That's very happy news."

She looked at Leo, who was, like Cat, smiling broadly. In his case she thought she saw something beyond a response to her congratulations: she saw pride; she saw self-satisfaction, perhaps even triumph. He looks like the lion who got the cream, she thought. The idea made her laugh.

"Yes, it's great news, isn't it?" said Leo. "And I reckon I'm one of the luckiest guys in Scotland."

Isabel caught Eddie's eye.

"I put some champagne in the fridge," Cat said, still holding out the ring for admiration.

"I'll open it," said Leo.

Isabel watched as Leo extracted the champagne and before he took the foil from the cork shook it vigorously, in the way of racing-car drivers celebrating a victory. There would be champagne all over the place as a result. Why do people do these things? Isabel asked herself. And then she rephrased the question: Why do they get engaged to people called Leo, who look like lions, and who shake perfectly good champagne bottles before they open them, in the misguided belief that shaking a champagne bottle is what one does?

But then she thought: Don't be so stuffy. **You** may not shake champagne bottles, but others did, and what was there to say that you were right and they were wrong? Nothing, she thought. Good form—whatever that might be—disapproved of just about everything; it was a paralysis of politeness. And what did it matter if Leo was a bit . . . a bit rough and ready? If he made Cat happy, then that was what counted. He was marrying Cat, not her.

The important thing was whether he would be a good husband to her niece.

It was the positive correction she needed. Now, taking a step towards Cat, she embraced her. "I'm very pleased for you," she said, willing herself to believe in the words she uttered. "I really am."

The champagne opened with an explosive pop, sending the cork flying through the air. Eddie dodged, but not fast enough, and the cork, with its restraining scaffold of wire, hit him just above the socket of his right eye. With a cry of surprise, Eddie doubled up, his hands shooting up to the site of his injury. Champagne and carbon dioxide spurted out of the bottle, drenching Cat and Leo and a customer who had come into the deli behind them. The customer let out a small scream of alarm as she saw a trickle of blood seep through Eddie's fingers.

"Not a good idea," said Leo, and laughed.

CHAPTER FOUR

❖

ISABEL TOOK Eddie to the Infirmary at Petty France, travelling with him in the back seat of a black cab. The taxi driver had arrived quickly, in response to her call, and was solicitous, even if he looked slightly concerned that blood might drip on his upholstery. He offered a box of tissues, but Isabel already had a large white handkerchief across which a red stain now spread like a tiny map of an island.

"Been in the wars?" the taxi driver said, looking in his rear-view mirror.

It was Isabel who answered. "A cork," she said. "He was hit in the eye by a cork."

The taxi driver shook his head. "I can't tell

you how many people I've driven to hospital over the years for that reason," he said. "Twenty? Maybe more. Comes with prosperity." He paused, and looked in his mirror again. "Champagne cork?"

Isabel nodded. "Not his fault," she said.

Eddie looked up from under the blood-stained handkerchief. "It definitely wasn't," he muttered. "It was him." And then for the benefit of the taxi driver, he said, "A real idiot called Leo. He's pure mental."

The taxi driver said nothing. Isabel touched Eddie's shoulder gently. "It was an accident, Eddie. I don't think Leo thought for a moment he might hurt anybody."

Eddie sat back in his seat, his right hand still pressing the handkerchief against his wound. He did not look at Isabel as he spoke. "That's what everybody says."

"Everybody?"

"Everybody says that when they do something stupid that hurts somebody else—even kills them. They say, **Oh, it was an accident. It wasn't my fault.**"

Isabel was cautious; Eddie was distraught,

and so she simply nodded. But then she added, "Try not to be too hard on him, Eddie. I think he probably feels pretty bad about it."

Eddie spun round to face her. With one eye covered, he blurted out, "Then why did he laugh?"

Isabel had to admit that Leo's initial reaction had been inappropriate. "Yes, that wasn't very nice. But then I think that people sometimes laugh out of nervousness. It's an odd human response to something that takes them by surprise. They don't mean it."

"He did," snapped Eddie. "He meant it."

"You're upset," said Isabel. "And understandably so. I think we shouldn't discuss it at this point. I'm sure that Leo will be very anxious about you."

It was no use. Eddie shook his head at this, causing a few spots of blood to fall on the seat. Surreptitiously, Isabel wiped them up with her own handkerchief. The driver, though, did not notice; he was coping with the traffic, and they were now approaching the turn-off to the Infirmary. "I'll drop you outside A&E," he said. "You can go straight in."

Isabel thanked him. Like many of the city's

taxi drivers, he was a social worker, psychologist and now ambulance driver all rolled into one. Suddenly he became more than that, and said, as he drew up outside the Accident and Emergency Department, "You have to give the other guy the chance to say sorry, you know."

Eddie did not respond, but Isabel smiled. "Thank you," she said. "And, yes, you're right."

"He can keep out of this," muttered Eddie, just loud enough for Isabel to hear him, but not the driver.

"Mind how you go, young man," said the driver.

They went into the Accident and Emergency Department. Lines of chairs filled most of the reception room; beyond these was a counter where the paperwork was done. Isabel led Eddie there, and gave the young nurse behind the counter his details.

"You're a relative?" asked the nurse.

Isabel briefly wondered what she was. Employer's aunt? Friend? "I work with him," she said.

The nurse noted something down. "What happened?"

Eddie found his voice. "A cork," he said. "Somebody hit me with a cork."

The nurse looked up. "An assault?"

Eddie nodded.

"No," said Isabel, as firmly as she could. "It was an accident. Somebody was opening a bottle of champagne and the cork hit him in the eye."

The nurse looked from Isabel to Eddie. "If this is a criminal injury, we have to note it down. There's a policeman on duty—you can have a word with him."

Isabel turned to Eddie. "Listen, Eddie," she said, "if you get the police involved in this, you'll just be making everything much more complicated."

Eddie shrugged, but remained silent.

Isabel tried another tack. "Bear in mind what Cat will think. Is she going to thank you for accusing Leo of assault? She was there, re-member; she knows it was an accident."

Eddie bit his lip. "Okay. I don't want to speak to the police."

The nurse looked at him intently. "Are you sure?"

"Yes, I'm sure."

"In that case," said the nurse, "take a seat. A doctor will look at you as soon as possible."

They found a place in the front row of chairs. Isabel was angry with Eddie, for his obduracy in blaming Leo for what had happened. Negligence, or even stupidity, might deserve some blame, but not the same measure of opprobrium that intentional wrongdoing merited. But she reminded herself of just who Eddie was, and why she should control her irritation. Eddie was vulnerable—a young man who had been damaged in a way that had never been made clear. He had made a great deal of progress—his confidence had grown by leaps and bounds—but there was a residual anxiety in his manner that could go some way towards excusing his reaction to what had happened. It had been an immature response, the sort of reaction one might expect of a child who could not distinguish between the intended and the unintended.

Eddie nudged her. He had lowered the handkerchief, and she forced herself to look at the wound. It was a laceration immediately above the eye, not far from the eyelid. She felt her own eyes water as she looked at it—a sympathetic response. **Sympathy**—the sentiment that lay at the very heart of the moral impulse, according to Adam Smith. This was the doctrine of sympathy that the Scottish Enlightenment philosophers had stressed; this watering of the eyes was the physical manifestation of the intellectual understanding of the pain of others; this was it, manifested right here in the Accident and Emergency Department of the Edinburgh Royal Infirmary. It was exactly that.

She stopped herself. This was not the time for philosophy—or was it? Might it not be that times of stress or suffering were precisely when philosophical issues became clearest?

Eddie nudged her again. "Look over there," he whispered.

"Where?"

He inclined his head in the direction of a man sitting a couple of rows behind them. "That guy with the jersey that says 'SCOTLAND.' Him."

Isabel looked. "What about him?"

"Look at his nose," Eddie said.

Isabel stared. It did not seem impolite—

in the circumstances, everybody in the waiting room was staring at the misfortunes of others.

Eddie was amused, and seemed to be struggling to contain himself. "He's got something stuck up his left nostril. Can you see it?"

Isabel could. From where she was sitting it looked like a large key—the sort of key used to wind a clock.

"It's a key, isn't it?" Eddie asked.

"It looks like it," said Isabel.

"How do you get a key stuck up your nose?" Eddie asked.

Isabel smiled. "Somebody might have been winding him up."

Eddie did not see the joke.

"Winding him up as in irritating him," Isabel explained. "You wind somebody up when you keep saying—"

"I know what that means," Eddie interjected.

"I'm sure you do," said Isabel. "And then that woman over there—see her? She keeps crossing and uncrossing her legs."

"Drugs," said Eddie. "She'll be needing a fix."

He was right, thought Isabel. With her

sheltered background, she had seen little of that, but Eddie would have, she reminded herself. Eddie came from a very different Edinburgh.

"Poor woman," said Isabel.

"Junkie," said Eddie.

"Yes, but we don't know how she ended up like that, do we?"

"She took drugs," said Eddie. "Simple."

"Yes, but . . ." She looked at Eddie. "Don't you feel sorry for people whose lives are a mess?"

"Yes, sure." He felt gingerly at his wound, provoking a further trickle of blood. "But the mess might be their own fault. Nobody made her take drugs, did they?"

"No, but—"

"So, there you have it. She did it herself. Now it's too late."

Isabel sighed. Eddie came from a disadvantaged background, and in such a place it was not uncommon to find unforgiving views on right and wrong. Perhaps it was only a prolonged education, coupled with the security it brought, that encouraged nuanced thinking. Isabel sometimes wondered whether liberalism was most enthusiastically practised by those who could afford it: you could be generous to others if the likelihood of your ever wanting for anything was remote; you could be kind to asylum seekers if they would never take up resources you would need yourself; you could be tolerant of crime if there was not much of it in your neighbourhood. And so on; and yet that was to dismiss the real arguments that the liberal position might muster— arguments that were nothing to do with self-interest, but were based on principle.

She was thinking of this when the nurse came over to call Eddie.

"We'll see you now," she said.

"I'll wait here," said Isabel.

Eddie hesitated, but then said, "I'd like you to come."

Isabel was touched. He was not much more than a boy, this young man; not much more than a boy who had had something traumatic happen to him in the past and who needed love and support.

"Of course," she said. And to the nurse, "May I?"

The nurse understood. "Absolutely," she

said. "We like to have friends or family around. Everyone needs somebody."

They were led to a cubicle. A young man—a medical student, Isabel thought—took Eddie's blood pressure and asked him about any medicine he was taking. Then he made a few notes and left. Somewhere in the background, in another of the curtained cubicles, a woman groaned.

"Is she having a baby, do you think?" Eddie whispered.

Isabel said she thought it unlikely. "A baby can be an accident, but they're usually not delivered in the Accident and Emergency Department," she said.

Eddie looked puzzled. "An accident?"

Isabel smiled. "An old-fashioned way of putting it. Never mind." She remembered what he had said of Rosie Mclaurin and her becoming pregnant in the cinema. That had been an accident, no doubt. Although one only became pregnant a little while after the event, she remembered being told in biology lessons at school: six or seven days, even more, she recalled. So Rosie Mclaurin might have embarked on the road to pregnancy during a showing of a **Star Wars** sequel, but the moment of conception could have been days later. Since she worked there, it might have been while she was serving popcorn, or it might have been later, when she was shoplifting with her friends in a supermarket. There were many unedifying possibilities.

"What's funny?" asked Eddie, as they waited for the doctor to come into the cubicle.

Isabel did not explain. It was too complicated, and anyway, Eddie did not find the same things amusing as she did.

The doctor came in. He did not speak to Isabel, and was brisk in his examination of Eddie.

"What did this?" he asked, as he examined Eddie's eye socket.

"A cork," said Eddie.

The doctor made a sound that seemed to express a mixture of distaste and resignation. "This happens too often," he said. "People should be more careful."

"That's what I think," Eddie said.

Isabel felt she had to say something. "It was an accident."

The doctor ignored this. "We'll take an

X-ray," he said. "I want to check that there isn't a fracture of the orbit." He touched Eddie's face gently. "That's this bit here—around your eye. Fortunately, the eye itself seems fine, but we'll need to check there's no haematoma behind the eye—that's bruising." He stood up. "They'll take you to X-ray. If the report is clear, you can go home. We'll put something on the wound, but it looks clean enough."

Isabel waited in the reception area while Eddie was taken off to the X-Ray Department. Half an hour later, he emerged from another door, a small dressing taped across his right eye.

"They said I can go home now," Eddie said. "But I want to go back to the deli."

Isabel was concerned. "Do you think you should?"

"They didn't say anything about not working."

She did not argue, but summoned a taxi on her phone. It arrived almost immediately, and they were back at Cat's deli about fifteen minutes later.

Cat was there, but Leo was not. Isabel was relieved about this, as she thought it better for

Eddie and Leo to say what they had to say to one another a little later on. Cat, though, had an apology to transmit. "Leo is really, really sorry," she said to Eddie. "He would be here to tell you that himself, but he had to go to see somebody. He asked me to tell you."

Eddie stared at the floor. It was obvious to Isabel that what she had said to him had not made the impression she had hoped. For her part, Cat waited for Eddie to say something, but when he did not, she frowned. This, thought Isabel, was not going to go away too quickly. She glanced at Cat, who raised an eyebrow enquiringly. Isabel made a gesture that she hoped conveyed the message that Eddie should be left to get over it in his own time.

"I'm going to stay," Isabel said to Cat. "I'll stay and help Eddie."

"You don't have to do that," said Eddie.

"I want to," said Isabel.

For the first time since the incident, Eddie smiled. "Thanks," he said.

She stepped forward and embraced him, realising, rather to her surprise, that she loved this young man, for all the unexpected things he said; she loved him as a mother might, or a sister, perhaps; she did not want him to be hurt, or disappointed, or frightened, or to feel any of the things that vulnerable young men might feel but be too uncertain, or simply too frightened, to say anything about.

SHE DID NOT SEE Jamie that evening until shortly after eight. He had a rehearsal at the Queen's Hall, and by the time he came home the boys were fast asleep, dinner— a ratatouille, as Jamie liked aubergines— was simmering in the oven and Isabel had poured herself a glass of New Zealand white wine. She had taken to allowing herself a glass of wine on alternate days of the week, with one becoming two on a Saturday. Jamie followed suit, although he would sometimes go for a pint of beer with members of the chamber orchestra with whom he occasionally played. That evening the rehearsal had finished at six-thirty, but the session in the pub, a hard-bitten **howff** on Causewayside, had lasted an hour. The conversation there had focused on the puzzling ways of a guest conductor whose interpretation of a Maxwell Davies piece they were playing was idiosyncratic in the extreme. "Max just didn't **mean** that," said a flautist, a woman with whom Jamie had studied at the Conservatoire. "If he had, he would have written something quite different. But he didn't."

In the kitchen, seated at her table, with a glass of wine and Auden's **Collected Shorter Poems** before her, Isabel exchanged with Jamie the news of the day.

"I don't know about you," she said, "but I have had a rather eventful twelve hours."

Jamie, having planted a kiss on Isabel's brow, sat in the chair beside hers. He stretched out and rested a hand on her shoulder—a gesture of gentle companionship that she loved. It was always his hand upon her shoulder, rather than hers on his—which meant nothing, she decided, other than that was the way it was. "That's the way it is" explained so much, she thought; it was a formula that could turn away impatience, disquiet, even wrath. That's the way it is. End of argument. **Finito.**

"Me too," said Jamie.

"You tell me then."

Jamie grinned. "I had a word with Freddie—you know, who conducts the school orchestra. I spoke to him about Mark Brogan."

Isabel laughed. "I thought you didn't want to."

"I didn't. But . . . Well, I wanted to get you off the hook. If his mother came along and tackled you about it, you'd be able to say that I'd done what they wanted."

"That was good of you," she said. "You shouldn't have, but thanks anyway."

"And you won't believe what happened," Jamie continued. "He said that both of the bassoonists in the orchestra are leaving. One is going to transfer to a school in Glasgow because the parents are moving, and the other is giving up music until after her exams next year. So . . ."

"So, two vacancies?"

"Yes. Freddie's heard Mark playing and he agreed that he's pretty dire, but he said that he could do some special simplified arrangements of the bassoon parts that should make it easier for him. He's going to take him."

Isabel laughed again. "**La Brosse** will be pleased."

He protested. "I thought that nickname was banned."

"The ban's been lifted."

Jamie said, "I've already had a beer. But I wondered if . . ."

"Have a glass of wine. You deserve it."

Jamie helped himself, and then asked Isabel about her day.

"First of all," Isabel said, "Cat's engaged. This morning. The ring was produced. And Leo too."

Jamie winced. "So that's still on?"

"It looks rather like it."

Jamie took a sip of his wine. "I've never been too keen on him. I don't know why."

Isabel agreed. She had harboured reservations about Leo all along, although he had helped her when somebody had made an attempt to intimidate her. That help, though, had been unconventional, and had involved Leo making a counter-threat, which had left her feeling uncomfortable.

"What is it?" Jamie asked. "Why do we both feel a little bit . . . lukewarm, shall we say?"

Isabel thought about this. "A different **Weltanschauung**?"

Jamie was unsure. "Lots of people have a different world view, but you still don't feel uneasy about them. You may think: **Well, I don't look at it like that,** but you don't think: **You come from another planet.**"

"Do you think that of him?" Isabel asked.

"He comes from . . . where was it? Kenya?"

"Yes. Not the real thing, of course. They were originally Scottish, I think—his grandfather was a professional hunter. And his father too, I think."

Jamie pointed out that he had met several people of that background, and had found nothing wrong with them. "I tend not to mind where people are from," he said. "They're just people first and foremost. The background bit is secondary."

"I agree," said Isabel. "No, I think it's his attitude. He's one of these people, I suspect, who believes in barging. You barge through things. You've no time for doubt. You charge. You shout a bit."

"Well," said Jamie. "She's made her choice. I suppose we'll have to accept it."

It was clear to Isabel that there was no alternative. You had to accept the choice of partner made by a son or daughter, or, as in this case, a niece. You had to. If you did not, then you lost that member of the family. That almost always happened when an unpopular choice was made: loyalty required that outcome.

"I'll make an effort," said Isabel. "In fact, I tried to be as welcoming as I could. You should have seen my insincerity—it was a breathtaking performance on my part. Academy award standard."

"Well done," said Jamie.

"And then," Isabel continued, "champagne was produced to mark the happy event, and that's when things went seriously wrong."

Jamie's eyes widened. "Somebody had too much? Things were said?"

Isabel shook her head. "It was even more dramatic than that. Leo shook the bottle before he opened it . . ."

Jamie let out a groan. "Why do people do that? What a waste!"

Isabel agreed and continued, "The cork came out like a bullet and hit Eddie in the eye—or just above it."

Jamie winced at this. He was squeamish about eyes, Isabel had noticed, and hated it when she asked him to put drops in Charlie's sticky eye. "Eyes are too close to where we are, if you know what I mean," he had said. "We're located somewhere just behind our eyes. In there, I think."

She told Jamie about the outcome; about the trip to the Infirmary and the conversation in the taxi. She said that Eddie was having difficulty in seeing the incident as an accident.

"Well, it wasn't **entirely** accidental," Jamie said. "It would have been different if he hadn't shaken the bottle and the cork had still come out too fast. That would have been a real accident."

Isabel accepted that there was a distinction, but she still maintained that if a consequence was not foreseen, then it might properly be described as an accident. Jamie listened to this, but was clearly not convinced. "I still think that Eddie has a right to feel angry," he said. "Leo caused the injury. He should have been more careful. Even if he didn't think that he could injure somebody, he **should** have thought about the possibility."

"Of course, he didn't handle the conse-quences very well," Isabel conceded. "To begin with, he laughed."

Jamie wrinkled his nose. "He's a pain, that guy. He's just so pleased with himself. Imagine laughing . . ."

"I thought it insensitive," said Isabel. "I don't think he intended to laugh." She paused. She was conscious of sounding a bit like a philosophy professor lecturing a class—but how else could one talk about philosophy? "Laughter is something we don't necessarily have control over."

Jamie looked doubtful. "Oh? Why not?"

"Because it's like a yawn . . . or a hiccough. Try controlling a yawn. Or a sneeze. And, any-way, look at the words we use—we **burst out laughing.** The word **burst** says it all. Laughter bursts out of you—you can't help it."

Isabel need not have worried about lectur-ing Jamie—he was enjoying this. "You can stop yourself laughing," he said. "I do it all the time when somebody like Mark Brogan plays the bassoon." He remembered something. "I once saw a clip from a Belgian television show. It was about people who had had unfortunate things happen to them in surgery. This poor man was being interviewed—he had a really peculiar voice, like Donald Duck's. Something had gone wrong in a throat operation. And the interviewer burst out laughing. And then somebody from the studio audience objected—in another very funny voice—and that made it worse. The interviewer collapsed in uncontrollable giggles."

Isabel smiled. It was a smile of sympathy, **à la** Adam Smith.

"The interviewer lost his job," said Jamie. "But apparently it was only an episode of a comedy show—not real life. Everyone was acting."

Jamie was grinning now at the recollection; and she was too. We can't help it, she thought. The misfortunes of others are often amusing. They just are, however much we know we should not find them so.

"I suppose we can't help ourselves," Isabel said. "A lot of humour involves nasty things happening to people. We laugh, although we shouldn't." She paused. "I was reading about the Rector of Stiffkey the other day. And I found myself laughing."

"What was so funny?"

"He was an eccentric English clergyman. He was very famous back in the 1920s and '30s for his mission to young actresses and showgirls in London. He took them back to his rectory in Norfolk for pyjama parties."

Jamie smiled. "A very kind man, obviously."

"Yes. Eventually he took to the stage at various seaside shows and circuses. He had an act that featured lions. They were tamed by young women he employed."

"Wonderful," said Jamie.

"Certainly colourful. But then he went into the ring one day and shouted at one of his lions—a lion called Freddie. Freddie objected, bounded over and started to eat the Rector of Stiffkey. And that was the end of him."

Jamie laughed. "In real life?"

Isabel nodded. "Nobody was acting."

Jamie laughed again.

"You see?" said Isabel.

"But that really **is** funny," Jamie said.

"Although very unfortunate."

Jamie agreed. "Yes, I suppose so." He became serious. "So, Eddie's in a huff?"

"He was. Whether he will remain in a huff, I don't know. But it's been an eventful day."

Jamie rubbed his hands. "Oh well, there are some things you can change, and some you can't. So, let's eat."

Isabel took the ratatouille out of the oven. She had been generous with the garlic, and it was obvious. But that suited Jamie, who could not get enough garlic, whatever the consequences.

"Do you mind if I smell of garlic?" he asked.

She did not, and so she answered his question with a request. "Will you play 'My Funny Valentine' after dinner? On the piano?"

"I could," he said. "But why?"

"Because of the words," she said.

He frowned. "Are they so special?"

"They're about somebody being just right," she answered. "The singer asks his valentine not to change a hair. He says she's perfect as she is, with all her imperfections."

"What's that got to do with smelling of garlic?"

"Everything," said Isabel.

After dinner, they went into the music room and Jamie sat down at the piano. He played "My Funny Valentine," and Isabel, a hand resting lightly on his shoulder, did her best to sing it. The words made her want to cry because they went to the heart of what it was to be in love: you thought the person you loved perfect as he was, she told herself, and in her case it happened to be true. Don't change a hair, Jamie—not a hair—not if you really care.

CHAPTER FIVE

❖

T HE NEXT DAY Isabel went for her dental appointment. Her dentist appeared to enjoy her visits, as he was a keen reader of a popular magazine, **Philosophy Now,** and would seek Isabel's view on some question raised in the latest issue. His current concern was the revival of interest in Stoic ideas. Did Isabel think that the Stoics were right in their cultivation of acceptance? Had she read Marcus Aurelius? Did she think that mindfulness was no more than a pale echo of ideas that the Stoics had long advocated? It was difficult for Isabel to answer, as a dental patient is always at a disadvantage in any discussion with the dentist, but she mumbled a few non-committal responses before he completed his check-up and issued a clean bill of health.

Her walk home after the appointment took her directly past Cat's deli, but she did not stop. Through the window she glimpsed Eddie engaged in serving a customer; the door of Cat's office was ajar, and Isabel imagined that she was at her desk. Eddie turned as she passed and caught sight of her outside; he waved cheerfully, and pointed to his eye. There was no sign of the dressing and she assumed that all was well. She waved back, gesturing to her watch to make the point that she did not have the time to call in. Eddie gave a friendly thumbs-up sign.

Back at the house, Grace had finished giving Magnus his lunch and was about to put him down for his early-afternoon rest. When she was in charge of the children, Grace made entries in a small notebook to record what had happened. Isabel glanced at this in the kitchen. **Charlie at school,** she read. **Magnus in bad mood. Kicked me on the shins. Told off, but didn't seem to care. Such a pity. Ate half an apple and almost an entire croissant. Nose a bit runny. Cleaned up.**

Isabel smiled as she read. Grace's narratives were pithy but managed to convey her feelings on the small events—the moods and desperations—of a young child's life. **Such a pity** was a particularly powerful comment, concealing a whole hinterland of disapproval. It would be Isabel's fault, Grace implied, that Magnus was impervious to the telling-off he had received, and if he grew up into a selfish adult, then it would not be hard to find the reason and blame accordingly: it would be Isabel's fault. Similarly, the fact that his nose was runny was not just a matter of report—it was a comment on the entire sanitary regime of Isabel's household. Children who came from better-ordered homes, it was implied, did not have runny noses or, if they did, those noses were better tended. **Cleaned up** would have been written with a sigh. The unspoken comment there was **Of course I'm the one who had to clean him up—yet again, because if I didn't do it, then it would never be done.**

She read the note, and smiled. Then, before she replaced the notebook in its customary place on a shelf of the Welsh dresser, she turned to an earlier entry at random. This had been written a few weeks earlier, when she and Jamie had been at a concert in Glasgow and Grace had babysat overnight. There had been an entry that she had meant to discuss with Grace, but that had slipped her mind. Now she was reminded.

Charlie wanted extra syrup at dinner. Gave him a small amount. Warned him that he would get fat and that fat boys could not play football. Isabel smiled at that. One did not say that to a child—at least not nowadays—but Grace was old-fashioned, to put it mildly. Then came an unexpected entry. **Charlie keeps talking about a friend called Tommy. I don't think Tommy exists. Has he spoken to you about him? He went on and on through bath-time. Tommy this, Tommy that.**

Isabel had meant to talk to Grace about this. She had not heard of Tommy, and was interested to know about him. He would be an imaginary friend, she thought—children often invented such people. She had forgotten about it, though, and made a mental note to raise it with Grace. What, if anything, did one do about imaginary friends? Did one encourage them, even to the point of joining in, or were they a private preserve of the child—a place into which adults should not intrude?

She made her way into her study. There was a pile of books for review, stacked up on her desk, each concealing between its pages a folded letter from the publisher. These letters followed a familiar formula: **I thought I might send you the enclosed book for review. This is an author that we are very honoured to have on our list and I am sure that you will enjoy this new look at this subject as much as I do.** Isabel dreaded these letters. Column space in the **Review of Applied Ethics** was limited, and in each issue she might be able to fit in, at most, four full reviews along with perhaps five or six "Briefly Noted" references to new books. That meant ten books in total might be mentioned, and since the **Review** was quarterly, that would make a total of forty books a year. Yet the number of books touching on philosophy published by the major English-language academic publishers in each year would far exceed that. How many? she wondered. Four hundred? And each of these would be the result of possibly years of work on the author's part; how much love and laughter and enjoyment of life would have been sacrificed for even one such book to appear? And then, when the book was eventually published and sent out to the editors of journals, there might be nothing but a deafening silence. Some books were not reviewed at all: nobody said anything about them, nobody put them on a list of recommended reading, nobody mentioned them on radio discussion programmes. There was just silence.

She sighed, and picked up the book on the top of the pile. This came from Princeton University Press and was a small volume on the subject of insincerity. That interested her. Princeton liked to publish pithy treatments of things that concerned people in their real lives, and insincerity was surely one such problem. She glanced at the author's name: it was a woman she had met at a conference the previous year. She remembered the meeting, as the author had said how pleased she was to have the chance to meet Isabel. Now it occurred to Isabel: Had she been sincere? She decided that she probably had, and, anyway, politeness did not amount to insincerity . . . except sometimes. We said, "How nice to see you," which was polite, even when we did not welcome the encounter. Surely there must be a category of justifiable insincerity, covering those social anodynes that people exchange simply to oil the wheels of daily life.

She decided that she would send **Insincerity Re-examined** out for review. But to whom? The thought occurred to her that it could go to Professor Lettuce. He was **substantially** insincere, Isabel thought, and it would be interesting to see what he made of the book. It would be a direct challenge to him—an affront, even. But then she thought: No, I can't do that because Robert Lettuce might write a biased review, and she would therefore be denying the author the chance of a fair hearing. She would have to rethink that.

She looked at the next book on the pile, and her heart sank. **Ukrainian Women Writers in Western Canada: The Philosophical Underpinning of the Prairie Imagination.** Accompanying this book was a gushing letter from the publishers, an obscure university press that Isabel had not encountered before.

It would be a university that was a long way from anywhere, she thought, and for a moment she imagined a white wood-board building on a quiet street in somewhere like Saskatoon, although it was not the University of Saskatoon itself, but somewhere else. And they would be so proud of this book, and of its author, who had trusted them to put it out into the world rather than go to one of the great presses in Toronto or Montreal. And just as well that she had taken that book there, because those great presses would have sighed and said that books on Ukrainian women writers did not sell particularly well these days—or ever, for that matter—and that much as they would have liked to be able to take this title on . . . And the author, this worthy, perhaps rather dull associate professor, would have gone home disappointed and reflected on how sad it was that people would not pay a modest price—thirty-seven Canadian dollars—for something that shed a whole new light on the Prairie Imagination.

She looked at the picture of the author on the book's back flap, and she caught her breath. There was a handsome-looking woman, with very fair hair, sitting bolt upright in a chair behind a desk. She had a strong face—a face that had seen suffering, Isabel thought, and the reason for that was immediately obvious. The professor was wearing glasses with heavily tinted lenses and beside her, propped up against a bookcase, was a white stick of the sort used by blind people.

Isabel looked more closely at the photograph, and noticed something else. The woman was an albino. That, she decided, would explain the problem with her sight. Restricted sight was a complication of albinism. So this professor had very poor sight.

She stared at the book. She would review this book. She had to. And she would do it herself, because she had no idea how she could possibly find somebody who knew anything about Ukrainian women writers in western Canada. She could find somebody, she imagined, by doing an internet trawl—there was always someone who knew something about any subject, somewhere, and you could find them with a simple enough search, but how would she be able to guarantee that this reviewer, whoever he or she turned out to be, would write a generous and encouraging review of the book? No, she could not, and so she would have to do it herself, and she would not stint in her praise. She would be as insincere as she needed to be, so that this woman in her distant prairie town might feel some delight at the fact that her book had been so well received by the **Review of Applied Ethics.** She would do that; she would write a good review because there were more important things than sincerity. And then it occurred to her that she could do more. Not only would she write a good review of **Ukrainian Women Writers,** but she would send to the professor the Princeton University Press book on insincerity and ask her to review that—only if she wanted to, of course—yet she could imagine that the professor would leap at the chance of a publication, even just a book review, in as prestigious a journal as the **Review of Applied Ethics.** Academics were always looking for opportunities to publish, and somebody who was still an associate professor might well have one eye on the **cursus honorum** along which she was expected to progress.

The doorbell rang and Isabel glanced at her

watch. Iain Melrose had been invited to arrive at three o'clock, and that was precisely what the time now was.

She showed him into her study.

"Please forgive the mess," she said, gesturing to her desk. "It's not always like this."

He laughed. "But I find mess comfortable. Piles of papers are . . . well, really rather human."

"Perhaps," said Isabel. "But then I find that if I go into somebody's office or study and find it all just so—nothing out of place, you know—I think: This is a sign of an organised mind. Papers all filed away. No clutter."

"Yes, but . . . ," said Iain, gesturing to the pile of books, "how uninteresting, don't you think? Isn't there such a thing as a creative mess?"

"Possibly," said Isabel. She thought of a conversation she had had with Edward Mendelson when he and Cheryl had been in Edinburgh last, and they had talked about the general messiness in Auden's domestic life. Edward, who acted as Auden's literary executor, had first met the poet when he lived in New York, in a flat on St. Marks Place.

"It was **very** insalubrious," Edward had

said. "All his living quarters were like that. The apartment in New York, the house in Austria. There were always great piles of books and papers all over the place—on the floor, on sofas, in corridors. And ashtrays full of cigarette stubs and letters and envelopes and so on."

He had paused. "And you've heard of Mrs. Stravinsky and the chocolate pudding?"

Isabel shook her head.

"Vera Stravinsky," Edward explained, "came to dinner with her husband when he and Auden were working on **The Rake's Progress.** She was dreading the lack of hygiene that she knew she would encounter in the flat. She went into the bathroom, which like everywhere in the flat was a terrible mess, and found a bowl of congealed substance on the cistern. Appalled, she put it into the toilet and flushed it away. It was, in fact, the chocolate pudding that Chester had made for the dinner and had put in the bathroom as that was the coldest place in the flat. Presumably the fridge was full or was too much of a mess."

Now, surveying her study through the eyes of her visitor, it occurred to her that, yes, even if it was untidy, it was **creatively** untidy. "Perhaps," she said. "But I'm still a bit ashamed of myself for not being tidier."

She invited Iain to sit down beside her on the sofa near the window. It was warm there, and a square of afternoon sun illuminated the cushion at one end of the sofa. It was a cushion featuring a reproduction of a hunting scene—a deer prancing through a forest, pursued by those elegant hunting dogs one sees in Flemish tapestries. She was not sure where the cushion had come from—it had belonged to her father, she thought, but she had no idea how he'd come by it or why he had wanted to have a hunting scene on his sofa.

Iain seemed relaxed. "It's good of you to see me," he said. "After all, not that many people would be prepared to hear out a perfect stranger coming up to them in a shop and making what is, after all, a somewhat unusual request."

Isabel smiled. "It's curiosity on my part," she said, adding, "Possibly."

"Not that I'm really a complete stranger," Iain went on. "I know we have a mutual friend in Guy Peploe, but there's something else. I actually knew your father—not very well, I'm afraid, but I met him on more than one occasion."

Isabel waited for him to continue.

"We fished together once," he said. "I had a friend who took a beat on the Tweed—down near Selkirk. He invited me to go down there once and there were two other rods. Your father was one of them. I remember that he caught a salmon—a large one. I caught nothing, as did my host.

"And then your father was friendly with an old friend of mine, the Honorary Polish Consul. No longer, of course, but you may remember him, I think."

Isabel did. "Angus?"

"Yes. Him. He was all sorts of things in town. Master of the Edinburgh Company of Merchants, I think. That sort of thing. And your father was his lawyer."

"I see."

"And then," Iain continued, "I discovered that my wife—my late wife—was a distant cousin of your father's. I only discovered this quite recently. I had heard about you, of course, although we had never met. And I thought that I should try to meet you at some point."

Isabel was silent. Iain had no idea of what he was doing in telling her all this: he was making it impossible for her to say no to the request he was about to make. Isabel had a theory of moral proximity that governed her decisions as to when she was obliged to act. Friendship between this man and her father would have been quite enough to trigger that responsibility, even without the addition of relatedness. Now this connection put it beyond any doubt. She was duty-bound to assist her visitor. Iain Melrose was within the sphere of moral proximity, and there was now a strong presumption that she would have to do what he asked of her, unless there was a very good reason to suggest otherwise.

Leaving him in the study, she fetched a tea tray with a teapot of freshly made Assam tea and a couple of mugs. She poured tea for both of them, and listened as he told her about himself.

"I should give you a bit of background," he said. "Just so that you know who I am."

She nodded. "I'd be interested."

"Actually, I've had a fairly uneventful life," he said. "I'm sixty-eight now."

"The years have been good to you," said Isabel. "No, I mean it. You don't look your age."

"Sixty-eight? Maybe—maybe not. I still go to the gym a lot. That helps."

"I must go," said Isabel. "I have a membership, but . . ."

"No need to give excuses. You look fine."

She took a sip of her tea. She glanced discreetly at her watch; she wondered how long this was going to take, but did not want to appear rude.

"I was a doctor," Iain continued. "I studied medicine at Aberdeen, although we came from Edinburgh—the family, that is. I was at school at Loretto, and then on to Aberdeen for medicine, as I've said. Then I came back to Edinburgh and worked here as a dermatologist. That was my career.

"I was married for forty years. We were very happy. And then I lost her. That was last year."

"I'm sorry," said Isabel.

"You get over it. Not entirely, perhaps, but

mostly." He paused. "I had a lot to keep me busy—and I still do, in fact. I've stopped practising, of course, but there's a family business that requires a bit of looking after. It's a woollen mill, actually—down in the Borders. We make a lot of cloth for kilts. I'm still the chairman."

Isabel said that she thought she might have visited the mill. "I bought some bolts of cloth, meaning to do something with them, but . . ."

Iain laughed. "A lot of people do that. It's the same with exercise bikes. I know an awful lot of people who have bought exercise bicycles that then, like them, gather dust."

"Good intentions," said Isabel. "And perhaps it's better to have good intentions that you don't act on than not have any good intentions at all."

Iain looked at her with admiration. "The fact that you say that sort of thing tells me that I've approached the right person," he said.

Isabel made a self-deprecatory gesture. "It's not hard to coin an aphorism," she said. "Anybody can do it. Putting them into effect is the difficult part."

"You see," he said, smiling. "Another aphorism—and a rather good one, if I may say so."

She steered the conversation back to him. "You said you were a dermatologist—why did you choose that specialty?"

"It's fascinating," he said. "The skin is an extraordinary substance—it really is. So, there's the technical challenge, and then there's the sheer pleasure of being able to offer most of your patients some relief. There are some branches of medicine where you can't do all that much—or where it takes a long time to get anywhere. Neurology, for example. There may not be all that much you can do in the case of some of the more devastating neurological conditions—and that's always hard for a doctor. Oncology used to be a bit like that, but now, of course, it's a very different story."

Isabel nodded. She knew a paediatric oncologist who said that his job had changed beyond all recognition from when he first started it. "I could do next to nothing then," he said, "but now . . ."

"Of course," Iain continued, "that's largely

thanks to the much-maligned pharmaceutical companies. You'll know the issue there, I imagine."

Isabel did. She had devoted an entire issue of the **Review** to the ethics of the pharmaceutical industry. She had taken what she considered an even-handed approach, but even so she had received more critical mail than on any other topic the **Review** had covered.

"There's a reason why they are much maligned," she said. "Their profits are much higher than in many other sectors. They argue they have to spend much more on research and development than other industries, but when you look closely at that . . ." She raised an eyebrow, wondering how her argument was being received. People had firm positions on this issue, and she was not in the mood to start a complicated technical argument over research-spending as a proportion of turnover. At the end of the day, the issue became one of simple compassion. Did you make a life-saving drug available to a person who could not afford it? Did you give it to them, or did you let them die?

It became apparent where Iain's sympathies

lay. "Oh, I agree," he said. "I was looking at something the other day that cost eighty thousand pounds a year. Eighty thousand. It doesn't cost that to produce, of course: the actual cost per pill must be pennies."

"But they have to get the research money back," said Isabel.

"Fair enough. But that should be recovered across the board. Standard non-life-saving drugs can do that. Painkillers, decongestants and so on." He paused. "Look, they can do their expensive research—and it **is** expensive—but they can cut their margins. They don't need to make twenty per cent. Very few firms can do that. And look at how much they spend on advertising and marketing. Billions and billions, at least in the case of the American pharma firms. Encouraging people to nag their doctors into giving them all sorts of drugs they probably shouldn't have."

Isabel sighed. There were some very imperfect corners of the world, and this, she thought, was one of them. Was it all the fault of capitalism, because capitalism was not so much concerned with need, or social responsibility, as profit? But if you went down that road in this particular case, then how did you answer the question of how many new drugs the planned economies of communism had produced? She did not know the answer, but she suspected it was very small. Profit motivated people; human need was less powerful a motivator. And freedom of research, of course, was another factor to be taken into account. The universities of communism were dull places on the best of days—havens for petty bureaucrats and ideologues, ready to go on for hours about how the principles of Marxism–Leninism should inform the work of scientists, but not too good at doing anything very constructive with a test tube.

It was Iain who ended the discussion. "Anyway, I didn't come here to burden you with my hobby horses," he said.

Isabel smiled. "I could give as good as I get," she said. "Don't ask me about restrictions on freedom of speech."

He laughed. "You do realise that what you've just said is oxymoronic, do you? **Don't speak to me about not being allowed to speak about something.**"

Isabel shared the joke. "Sorry. But you know what I mean."

"And I won't," he said. "May I tell you a bit more about myself?"

She inclined her head. Her interest had been piqued, and she was keen to find out more.

"Helen—that's my wife—and I lived up near the Hermitage of Braid. I'm still in the house up there. It's far too big for me, but I've no desire to move. And we had an estate up in Argyll. I still have that." He hesitated. "That sounds a bit boastful, I know. Listing one's possessions, so to speak."

"Not necessarily," said Isabel. But she knew what he meant: there was a fairly strong convention that you did not make too much of what you had. It was regarded as being tactless when there were people who had so little. **Don't show off** was ancient advice that parents gave to children, but it was perfectly sound. Of course, there were cultural variations: in Sweden it was the height of bad taste to disclose how much money you had; in Russia of the old Soviet Union it was not in the slightest bit rude to ask somebody what their salary was. Perhaps that had survived the end of the Soviet era; perhaps that was why the Russian oligarch she had been reading about in a newspaper feature should not be embarrassed by having such a showy private yacht.

She remembered what she had been told about the entry of this yacht into the waters of the west coast of Scotland. The owners had anchored in a bay and then sent a member of the crew ashore to engage children to play with their children. Isabel had been struck by the poignancy of this; by the image of the small Russian children, socially isolated because they lived and travelled in such splendour, nonetheless wanting to play with ordinary children. And she imagined what might have happened; how the Russian children had joined in a game proposed by one of the Scottish children, but had expected to win it. And the Scottish child had resisted this and had insisted on his deserved victory, to find himself being seized by the Russian children's bodyguards and taken off the boat. Perhaps it had not been like that at all; the rich are no different from anybody else, as Mary Colum told Hemingway—they just have more money.

"The reason why I tell you all this," Iain said, "is that it is precisely these things that I possess that are causing me anxiety."

"That's not uncommon," observed Isabel. "The burdens of wealth are well known."

"Yes, perhaps. And I know that I could simply divest myself of just about everything I have, and still have enough for myself, of course."

"You could," said Isabel. "A lot of people seem to experience a sense of elation when they give things away. They feel lighter, I'm told. It's a clearing of the decks."

Iain stared at her. "But if I did that," he said, "I would have to choose among a number of people who all probably think that they are the ones who should get their hands on my place up in Argyll. That choice wouldn't be an easy one, and it would leave several people very unhappy."

"Divide it then," said Isabel. "Divide it strictly pro rata, or whatever the expression is. Equal shares for everybody."

Iain shook his head. "You can do that with money," he said. "But you can't do that with land. If you divide it and sell off portions, it ceases to be the thing it was. It won't work. That's why primogeniture was invented. Do you get my drift?"

"Yes. Yes, I do."

"And there's another thing," he continued. "Running a Highland estate is no picnic financially. These places gobble up money—if you want to run them well."

"And you do, don't you?"

Iain nodded. "Yes, I want that bit of Scotland—that's the way I look at it, you see—I want that bit of Scotland to be preserved and cherished. That's taken a lot of money—most of the money I get from my investments, as it happens. And the woollen mill. It all goes into deer fencing and tree planting and using proper lime to point the walls of the walled garden—and so on. Every penny I've earned has been spent on that place. Every penny—more or less."

Isabel was familiar with that attitude to land ownership. It was regrettably rare, but it tended to surface when it came to these large Scottish estates. It was an attitude of stewardship that was quite at odds with a profit-based approach to land. You did not mine the land; you nurtured it.

Iain explained that there were two areas of life in which conflict was almost inevitable: land and succession. "People can fight with one another for generations over those things," he said. "That's why I'd prefer the decision as to who gets what to be taken by somebody other than me—and revealed only after my death. I won't be around to get the flak, and if the decision is made by an outsider, on defensible principles, then it will be better all round."

"I think my father ran family trusts like that," said Isabel. "He had clients who preferred him to make the decisions as to who got what." She thought of her own trust, and of the role of Hamish MacGeorge and Gordon MacGregor. She remembered how, at the two most important meetings of the trust each year, one of them—she thought it was Gordon—invariably brought a bottle of sherry and a soda-water syphon with him, and how, at the end of the meeting, he would offer everybody a glass of this curious mixture. She always said no; she did not like sherry all that much, although she could drink it when the occasions of politeness demanded it. Hamish beamed at the suggestion and always said, predictably on cue, "One of Spain's great contributions to civilisation." To which Gordon would make the same reply, year after year, "Let us not forget about Francisco Pizarro, Hamish. The **conquistadores,** you know . . ."

This brief exchange—which never went any further, at least in Isabel's presence—was accompanied by the hissing of the soda-water syphon. And then the conversation would drift off in another direction altogether. Both Hamish and Gordon were keen exponents of Scottish country dancing, although their wives were not. This meant that the two of them sometimes went off on country-dancing expeditions as a twosome, sometimes ending up dancing in exotic locations: men could dance with other men in Scottish country dancing and indeed the Reel of the 51st Highland Division, one of the most famous of the Scottish dances, had been devised by Scottish army officers in a German prisoner-of-war camp during the Second World War. They had all been men, of course, and had coped with the tedium of their existence by working out the elaborate steps of a regimental dance. The detailed choreography of this dance had been set out in a letter home written by the reel's originator, but the Germans had intercepted this letter and spent much time and energy trying to crack the code that they thought it represented.

Hamish and Gordon had regaled Isabel with an account of the visit of what they called their "dance circle," an eighty-strong Scottish country-dancing team, to Istanbul, where they had given an exhibition performance at the Pera Palace Hotel. And then there had been the year when they had travelled to Russia and had danced at an event organised by the British Council and the British Embassy. "Scottish country dancing is a good example of what they call **soft power**," Gordon had said. "Soft power is all about influence. That's what they said at the embassy. That's why they liked us."

Hamish nodded his agreement. "The other embassies were green with envy," he said. "There had been talk of the President of

Russia coming along to take part, but it didn't happen. The First Secretary at the embassy told me that he did that sort of thing—show up at events, anything from biker rallies to the Bolshoi—in order to get a photograph of himself for his annual calendar."

"He publishes a calendar, you see," said Gordon. "It shows him in various places— wrestling with bears and so on . . ."

Hamish wagged an admonitory finger. "He would **never** do that," he scolded. "He'll be on very good terms with bears."

"And then we went to India," Gordon went on. "Jaipur, where we danced at the Pink Palace, and made a very big stir—and then that wonderful place on the . . . What was the name of that holy river, Hamish? The . . ."

"Narmada," supplied Hamish. "We were guests there of that nice man Richard Holkar. You'll have met him, Isabel."

Hamish and Gordon both assumed that Isabel, whom they regarded as well connected, knew everybody.

Isabel shook her head. "I haven't, I'm afraid."

"You'd like him," chimed in Gordon.

"Richard is the son of the last Maharaja of Indore. The maharaja had a daughter by his first wife—she's the current maharani—and then he married a second wife, an American. So, Richard is half American and half Indian. He's one of the most interesting men in India."

"The family was fabulously wealthy, of course," said Hamish. "The maharaja had a very large jewel collection. They loved jewels, those fellows."

Gordon was reminded of something. "Who was that Indian prince who had so many jewels he couldn't possibly wear them all? So he had a servant who walked behind him—wearing the extra jewels for him."

Hamish could not remember who that was. "I don't think it was this maharaja. This one had a rather strange Bauhaus-style palace in Indore itself. That was sold, and the government of India took an awful lot of their stuff under various tax agreements and so on. But Richard is still in this wonderful fort—as a tenant, I believe. He runs it as a really good hotel—very quiet and unfussy. Just perfect in every respect. It was where his great-grandmother lived . . ."

"Several more greats-grandmother," corrected Gordon. "Ahilyabai Holkar. An early feminist—well before the invention of modern feminism."

"There have always been powerful women who have spoken up for women," said Isabel. "It's nothing new."

"Of course not," said Hamish, hurriedly. "There's a statue of her at the entrance to Richard's fort. Pilgrims come every day and bedeck it with flowers. Every day, Isabel. Can you imagine anybody here bothering to do that?"

"Anyway," said Gordon. "We danced there and it went down really well. We always take a couple of pipers with us, and they went up to the top of the fort and played 'Mist-Covered Mountains.' The Indians were in **floods** of tears. They just love that sort of thing."

They lapsed into silence. Then Hamish said, "Our last event on that particular trip was up in Nepal. We went up to Pokhara, where they have this big Gurkha recruitment base, Isabel, and we stayed there at Tiger Mountain Lodge. Marcus Cotton runs that—you must know him, Isabel?"

Isabel shook her head. "Alas, no."

"The Gurkhas love Scottish country dancing," said Gordon. "They sent a team up to the lodge—you can just imagine them, with their kukris and everything. They showed us some of their special Gurkha dances. Many of them were just slightly different versions of the standard dances—Dashing White Sergeant, and so on. But some were new to us."

"Marcus invited a Dutch friend of his to come along to our event. George van Driem."

"I don't think I know him," Isabel said quickly.

"No, perhaps not. You should meet him, though."

"That would be nice," said Isabel.

"He became a botanist and then went on to become a linguist," Gordon continued. "He was appointed to a chair at a Swiss university, which is where he is now."

"And he wrote a book on the history of tea," Gordon interjected. "Not just the history—everything about tea. Everything."

"He went to Nepal for his linguistic research rather than as a botanist," said Hamish. "He had spent a lot of time researching Himalayan languages. He actually discovered two previously unknown languages, Isabel. Two! And wrote grammars for a number of others."

"George came to dinner," said Hamish. "And we had a fascinating conversation . . ."

Isabel became aware that Iain Melrose was staring at her.

"Thinking of something?" he asked.

She returned to the present moment. Hers was a particular form of consciousness, she thought: not a stream of consciousness but a meandering, deltoid consciousness, in which memories and speculations—fantasies, even—rubbed shoulders with awareness of the present. "Daydreaming," Jamie had said, smiling. "Not so sexy a name for it, but that's what it is."

Iain became business-like. "I'm taking up too much of your time. I'd like to be specific about my proposal. I'll nominate you as my executor—if you accept, of course. In return I shall make provision for a reasonable sum, not a vast amount of money—let's say five thousand pounds—to be—"

She interrupted him sharply. "I would not do this for payment."

"What I was going to say, if you had let me finish . . ." It was a mild rebuke, and he must have regretted it immediately, as he looked apologetic. "What I wanted to say is that this money would be available for you to donate to whatever cause you wish."

She looked at Iain. This was a good man— that was perfectly apparent. He was not a complete stranger to her, as there were shared friends that made their circles of moral proximity intersect. And now there was this additional element to consider: a charity would benefit substantially if she were to agree.

She decided out of habit. She had been brought up to do the right thing. She had spent years of her life worrying over what was right and what was wrong. This was obviously right. "I'll do it," she said. And then she added, "Of course I hope that I shall not be required to act for a very long time."

Iain smiled at that; a rueful smile, she thought, and she sensed, immediately, what was coming next. "Unfortunately, that's not the case," he said, his voice even. "I'm living on borrowed time, I'm afraid. I won't burden you with the details, but I have stage-four cancer—fairly widely disseminated. Oddly enough, I'm still pretty much asymptomatic, but it's still too late for them to do anything, really; they might have been able to do something until a few months ago, but not now."

She lowered her eyes. "I'm very sorry," she said.

"Thank you. But I'm fairly resolved about it. I've had a good life, on the whole. I've been fortunate—I had a wonderful marriage. I had the great good fortune of having a circle of amusing and loyal friends. What is there for me to regret?"

He seemed to be waiting for an answer, and so Isabel said, "Nothing, I suppose, except the thought that you may no longer—" She broke off. It was awkward. It was not easy to talk about somebody's death when that person was sitting in front of you.

"No, go on," he urged. "Say what you wanted to say. I'm not squeamish about death. And you don't need to creep around the issue with me."

"All right. What I was going to say was that you will no longer be here to experience the world that I assume you love. The familiar things of your life. Your friends. Your place up in Argyll. It must be hard to say goodbye to all that."

He agreed. "Absolutely, that's the only hard bit. I think of it as **dying when the world still seems precious—when the world still seems beautiful.** I know that sounds a bit obscure, but that's what comes to my mind."

"There's a folk song that puts it rather well, I think. There's a line about how hard it is to die when all the birds are singing in the sky. I think that says it, don't you?" said Isabel.

He looked at her mutely, and she wondered whether, in accepting his invitation to speak freely about death, she had nonetheless crossed some ill-defined border. But she had not, because after a few moments he said that he knew the song and that it rang true. " 'Seasons in the Sun.' Of course, the man who wrote it—and I can't remember his name—was a young man at the time and can't have known that particular regret. He had obviously imagined it rather poignantly, but he did not actually **know** it."

"But surely that's what art is," said Isabel. "The envisaging of the reality of another."

"Possibly." He glanced at his watch, and she thought: How much more significant does that become when you know your time is limited? "So, I'm afraid accepting this executorship will not be a theoretical undertaking for the future—it's about some time . . ." He shrugged. "Some time rather soon."

Again, she said, "I'm sorry. I really am very sorry."

He became business-like once more. "Now, as to the potential beneficiaries: we had no children, and neither my wife nor I had siblings, so the closest relatives are three cousins—and not very close ones. They are the people for whom the testamentary trust is intended." He paused. "I'd like you to meet them. They all live in Edinburgh, so there will be no difficulty about anybody being too far away."

"All right."

"I'll give you all the details in due course and make some arrangements." He rose to his feet. Looking about him, he nodded towards a painting on the wall beside one of Isabel's bookcases.

"That painting . . ."

Isabel followed his gaze. It was a large

James Cowie watercolour—a rural scene from north-east Scotland. It had belonged to Isabel's father, who had been given it by one of Cowie's pupils. She had grown up with that painting and remembered how, as a small girl, she had been held up to look at it closely by her mother. The painting now had a scent to it, in Isabel's mind—the scent of her mother's perfume, which she had experienced as they had both looked at it. That had been a perfume that her mother bought from a small **parfumerie** in Lyon. Isabel had tried to trace it much later, well after her mother's death, and had failed. A letter sent to the address she had found in an old address book came back stamped **Deceased.**

"It's a Cowie, isn't it?" Iain said.

"Yes. Painted in 1925. It's an Angus scene, I think, although I don't know exactly where. Somewhere near Arbroath. He taught at Hospitalfield, as you probably know."

Iain nodded. "I love his work. That painting he did—**A Portrait Group**—in the Gallery of Modern Art, is just so haunting. I can stand in front of it for hours."

He looked back at Isabel. "One of the

cousins," he said, "is an artist. He has an opening coming in a couple of days. Would you like an invitation? It's at Guy's gallery, as it happens. Perhaps . . ." He looked at her enquiringly, and seemed pleased when she agreed to go.

"The other two are quite different," Iain said. "One is a property developer. She's called Sarah. The other is a rather quiet man— I think you'd like him—called John."

"Will the cousins know about my being the executor?"

He replied that they would. "I prefer openness, and so I propose to drop them all a note later on today." He paused. "As long as you don't mind."

Isabel assured him that she did not. She could not see any reason to conceal what her enquiries were all about. Of course, that meant that some of the beneficiaries might tailor their responses to what they thought would stand them in best stead, but she imagined that would be fairly obvious. Isabel had always prided herself on her ability to sniff out insincerity, and she suspected that she was about to be exposed to a good dose of exactly that. But she had agreed to act—that was the important thing—and she would make the best job of it. As she accompanied Iain to the front door, where they said goodbye, she thought: This is a judgement of Paris.

The thought amused her. She was Paris, and as in the myth there were three contestants, and she had one golden apple to award. And then she thought of the consequences. The original judgement had led to the Trojan War.

She looked out after the figure of Iain, now retreating down the street. It was not too late to run after him and tell him she had changed her mind. She could do that quite easily, but . . . She faltered. There was no doubt as to where her moral obligation lay: it was to help this man who was trying to achieve something laudable, but needed assistance to do it. She could not turn down someone who had a short time to live: How could anyone do anything like that?

Yet they did, she told herself, and the thought caused her pain. People were quite capable of being uncharitable, even merciless, to those whose mortality was writ large. And yet the bleakness was alleviated here and there by

enlightenment. There were compassionate release rules that allowed terminally ill prisoners
to be released to die in dignity. Isabel had received an article about the ethics of that issue:
the peer assessment had been ambivalent,
with one reviewer labelling the article "largely
derivative." That had moved Isabel to reject
it, although she tried—as was her practice—
to be as positive about it as she could. She
said that she had read it with **enormous** interest: that was true, and she hoped that this
might be some consolation to the disappointed author. Then, three months later, she
heard from one of the author's colleagues—
a regular book reviewer for the **Review**—
that the author of "Compassionate Release:
Deciding When Is Late Enough" had herself
just died, after a long battle with illness.

That had been a coincidence, of course,
and she had no reason to reproach herself.
But there being no grounds for self-reproach
did not mean an end to guilt. Feelings of
guilt might be deserved, but, almost as often,
might not be deserved at all—it depended on
whether you were susceptible to guilt. Many
psychopaths were happy for precisely that

reason—they led guilt-free lives. Many saints, by the same token, felt guilty throughout their saintly lives. Isabel was aware of where she was on that particular spectrum: she felt far more guilt than she should, and she knew that she should do something about it. But she had not yet tackled the issue, and that, like the pile of books in her study, like the gym membership bought but not used, like the failure to **like** Leo in the way that she would like to be able to do—that certainly brought guilt. She closed her eyes, took a deep breath and held it in before releasing it slowly through her nostrils rather than her mouth. Perhaps yoga was the answer.

CHAPTER SIX

❖

ON MONDAY MORNING Jamie left the house early in order to be in Glasgow for a rehearsal at nine-thirty. Isabel took Charlie to nursery school at George Watson's College, only a few streets away from the house, before delivering Magnus to the nearby playgroup where he occasionally spent the morning. Charlie had now settled into his nursery class, although it had not been easy at the beginning. Leaving him with the teachers had involved a programme of distraction and promises, during which time Isabel would slip away as discreetly as she could manage before Charlie realised she was not there.

"He has a good set of lungs on him," said

one of the teachers, cheerfully. "And he always manages to land a few well-placed kicks."

Isabel was mortified by this comment, although she understood that Charlie was not the only four-year-old to throw uninhibited public tantrums. "I'm so sorry," she said. "We try, you know."

"Of course you do," said the teacher. "And we do want them to be little individuals, don't we? It wouldn't do to wring all the character out."

Isabel nodded. She was all for self-expression, except where the self so expressed would be better unheard. And there was still a duty incumbent upon parents to **civilise** their offspring—to make them fit for human society. There was nothing worse than an undisciplined little brat—not that Charlie was anywhere near that yet. She was trying to teach him not to bite other children, but it was not a lesson that he seemed particularly interested in learning.

She had read in a child-rearing manual that a highly effective way of dealing with biting was to put mustard in the child's mouth whenever it occurred. "This invariably works very well," wrote the author, a paediatrician from Toronto, "but it is not a course of action that we can recommend. In fact, we completely dissociate ourselves from such practices—even if they are highly effective." To which the publisher had added a note in these terms: **Please note that this approach is not endorsed by the author of this book, nor by the Canadian Paediatric Association.**

Isabel had laughed. There were ways of giving people information while at the same time keeping one's distance. **Should you wish to blow open a safe, this is what you would do—not that we in any circumstances advocate safe-blowing . . .** She had tried reasoning with Charlie, but had not got anywhere. She had tried a system of positive reinforcement, promising a small chocolate bar at the end of each week in which no biting incident was reported. That, too, had failed. And so she had decided that she would secretly put just a small dab of hot mustard in Charlie's mouth when she saw him biting Magnus or the next time she received a biting report from school. And it had worked. He had howled and stamped his feet in rage, but the cause-and-effect message had clearly been received.

She was embarrassed by this success of old-fashioned punishment. If she were reported to the authorities, she would no doubt be spoken to severely by the social work department or even by the procurator fiscal. She could be prosecuted, and the details of her trial splashed all over the front page of the **Scotsman.** She imagined the pleasure that would give Professor Lettuce, who would no doubt write to the other members of the **Review**'s board and offer to take over the chairmanship in the light of "Ms. Dalhousie's most regrettable lapse of judgement and her subsequent conviction for violence."

Of course it could put Charlie off mustard for life, and only later, perhaps, the memory might come back to him of his mother approaching with a small teaspoon of yellow paste and forcing it through his gritted teeth like a medieval poisoner. He might even raise it with her, and draw her attention to the trauma she had caused him. "I know I've got a lot to be grateful for," he would say, "but

I've always felt that there's something about mustard . . ."

She would have to say sorry. She would say, "But you were a terrible biter, darling, and I had to stop it. You can't go through life biting people—you just can't."

She returned to the house. Grace would go to collect the children at half past two, and this gave her almost five uninterrupted hours in which to deal with the backlog of work in her study. She had a long list of emails to send, a pile of books and papers to send out to reviewers—Isabel insisted on sending hard copy—and several future contributors to contact. The printer's bill had to be settled, and a few other random invoices attended to. Five hours would not be enough for all of this, but it would enable her to make a start.

Of course she knew that a coach and horses could be driven through her plans if Cat should suddenly phone up from the deli with a request for help. And she had decided to be firm in dealing with that call, if it came, and to say, "I'm sorry, I'd like to help, but I'm just too busy." The words were ready, but it was not just finding the right words that was required—it was summoning the resolve to utter them in the face of one of Cat's pleas.

When the phone rang, it was not Cat, though, but Hamish MacGeorge. In her relief at not hearing Cat at the other end of the line, Isabel greeted Hamish particularly enthusiastically. "It's really nice to hear from you," she said.

The lawyer seemed taken aback by the greeting. "Well," he said in his slightly prissy accent, "I would say the same to you, except it is I who am calling you, rather than you calling me." She heard him drawing a breath at the other end of the line. In the background she thought she could make out office noises—a printer starting up, the drawer of a filing cabinet being slammed shut.

She waited.

"We need to have a meeting of the trustees," he said. "And sooner, rather than later."

She felt a sudden tug of concern. The market was a fickle place; the value of investments could go up in smoke before fund managers could do a thing. Computers, operating sales according to their own plans and logic, could wipe out whole enterprises simply by issuing an instruction to sell. This had not happened to the trust before, but she occasionally reminded herself that it could.

"Is the market misbehaving?" she asked.

"Oh no," said Hamish. "Far from it, in fact. The market is doing very nicely and we are very well balanced—for the most part. No, what I think we need to discuss is a request I've had from your niece. She's put in an application for funding."

Isabel relaxed. "Yes," she said. "I encouraged her to do that."

This brought silence. Then, "To put in this particular application?"

Isabel tried to remember what exactly Cat had said. It was "something for the business," she seemed to recall. A new refrigerator unit, she thought; the existing one was making a labouring sound and would shortly need a new compressor, she imagined. It would be easier to replace it than to arrange an expensive repair.

"She didn't tell me exactly," she said to Hamish. "I wouldn't be surprised if it's for a new fridge."

There was another silence. Then Hamish said, "I see."

Isabel frowned. Had Cat chosen a particularly expensive refrigeration unit? They could cost thousands.

Hamish continued. "A Porsche Cayenne," he said. "Turbo. New. Out of the box, if that's what these expensive toys come from."

Isabel caught her breath. Then she said, "That's a car, I take it."

"Yes," said Hamish. "It's a very expensive SUV. In fact, I've looked at the price list and I see it comes in at just over one hundred and ten thousand pounds." There was outrage in his voice—Presbyterian outrage that went right back to the seventeenth century.

"I don't know what to say," said Isabel.

"That's why we need to meet," said Hamish. "And we need to meet this morning, I think, because Cat tells me in her message that her new fiancé, a certain . . ." His voice trailed away as he consulted his papers. "A certain Leo has booked a test drive this afternoon and is keen to do the deal by lunchtime tomorrow."

Isabel closed her eyes. She tried yogic breathing: inhale through one nostril, exhale through the other. But there is a limit to what yogic breathing can achieve, and she found herself thinking, absurdly, of a yoga master's car that would inhale air though one exhaust and exhale it through the other. But the shock she felt was too much for such levity, and she put the thought out of her mind.

THEY MET at the lawyers' office shortly after eleven. When Isabel was shown into the client meeting room, Hamish and Gordon were already there, poring over a file of papers. A tray of coffee was produced by the receptionist who had accompanied Isabel to the room. A plate of shortbread fantails was already on the table.

"Our firm used to act for a big biscuit manufacturer," said Hamish, offering Isabel the plate. "We continue to have their shortbread available."

Isabel took a piece. There was something quintessentially Edinburgh about this meeting, with the two rather old-fashioned and pernickety lawyers, and the plate of shortbread.

"I'm sorry about the lack of notice," said Gordon. "But, as Hamish explained, we've been rather bounced into this."

"Or rather," said Hamish, "there has been an **attempt** to bounce us into something." He looked down at a paper in front of him. "One hundred and ten thousand pounds. One hundred and ten!"

Gordon shook his head. "That rather nice car of yours, Isabel—I wonder how much that's worth."

"My green Swedish car?" She shrugged. "Five thousand, perhaps. Although I think that cars like that eventually start to appreciate. Some of these vintage cars are astronomically expensive."

"They certainly are," agreed Gordon. "Our executory department recently had a valuation for a car they found in a deceased client's garage. Seventy-five thousand for an MG sports car that didn't even start."

"That's right," added Hamish. "One of our trainees tried to get it going—he knows about these things. But everything had been seized, I think. Yet that was the evaluation for inheritance tax purposes."

"I would never pay that for a car," said Isabel. "I don't see the point."

"Rarity," said Gordon. "If something is

rare, people want it and will pay what's needed to get it. It has nothing to do with utility."

"Which brings us to the topic in hand," Hamish said. "This application from your niece." He gestured towards a typed letter in the file.

Isabel asked to see it, and quickly scanned the single page. Cat had not wasted her breath. "I would like to apply for funding from the trust for a business purpose," she wrote. "I currently have no vehicle to use for the deli. As Isabel will confirm, I have to collect food-stuffs from time to time and also visit my suppliers at their premises. I think, therefore, that an SUV will be best suited for this purpose. I have looked at the various models and feel that a Porsche Cayenne Turbo is probably best for me. It is a very functional car."

She put down the letter. "Well!" she exclaimed. "She makes the point succinctly— you have to give her that."

"But, my goodness, a Porsche!" objected Hamish. "She needs a Ford Transit van. That's what businesses like hers use."

"Yes," said Isabel. "That would be more sensible. But then . . ." She hesitated. This was family business, and she was not sure whether she wanted to involve Hamish and Gordon in a discussion of her misgivings. But she decided that she would have to.

"Far more sensible," Hamish repeated.

Isabel sighed. "As you know, Cat has just become engaged." She paused again.

Hamish glanced at Isabel and then said, in a tentative tone, "Might we assume that an engagement could be a sign of her settling down—which is good, of course, bearing in mind . . ." He waved a hand vaguely, signifying, Isabel imagined, Cat's past, with its landscape of discarded boyfriends.

"I'm positive about it," said Isabel, thinking, Yes, I am: I'm positive because I've decided to make the best of this, and because I have no alternative. But then she thought: A Porsche Cayenne?

It was obvious whose idea that was. And, what was more, it was unambiguously suggestive of gold-digging. Leo must correctly have worked out that somewhere in Cat's background there was money, and this was his opening gambit.

She cleared her throat. "I said I'm positive—

perhaps I should have said I **was** positive about her engagement. This, I'm afraid, changes the picture completely."

Both Hamish and George understood exactly what she meant.

"This young man," said Hamish. "Do you know anything about him? About his background?"

Isabel told them what she knew. "He was brought up abroad," she said. "His father lived—still lives, I think—in Kenya, but he was, I think, a Scot. Leo went to school in Cape Town, I think, or somewhere like that, and then ended up back in Scotland."

It was obvious to Isabel that neither Hamish nor Gordon approved of this. Leo's background made him an unknown quantity to them—somebody well outside the normal experience of bourgeois Edinburgh.

"Some of these chaps," Gordon said, "can be a bit wild, so to speak. They're used to wide open spaces and so on."

Isabel had to suppress a smile as she imagined an encounter between Leo and Gordon. "That's true, I suppose. But I don't think we should put too much store by stereotypes."

Both Gordon and Hamish were a picture of injured innocence. "Of course not," said Gordon. "One must be open-minded."

"Exactly," said Hamish.

They looked at Isabel expectantly. She thought: But, Hamish and Gordon, you are such wonderful stereotypes yourselves.

"It seems that this request," she said, "has been inspired by Leo. It looks as if he has decided that this is his chance to get hold of a fancy car at somebody else's expense."

Hamish shook his head. "It's the sort of thing trustees have to be particularly vigilant about."

Gordon agreed. "We have our battles to fight, believe me. Youngsters make outrageous requests to family trusts every day of the week. Trustees have to be firm."

"So, we say no?" asked Isabel.

Hamish looked at Gordon, and then at Isabel. "Would you like us to do the necessary? We can tell her formally that the trust hasn't approved the request."

Isabel considered this, but then she decided that if there was dirty work to be done, then she should not pass it off. As if anticipating this response, Gordon assured her that this sort of thing was no trouble to them. "It's what we're paid to do. We can dress a refusal up in all sorts of legal language."

"We can throw in a few Latin phrases too," added Hamish. "That usually silences people. **Ceteris paribus, animus contrahendi,** etc."

Isabel laughed, and there was a relief of tension. "No, I'll speak to her directly. I'll tell her that we thought the vehicle in question inappropriate for a variety of reasons. But I take it I can say that the trust would be prepared to buy her a modest van?"

"Yes," said Gordon. "Let's say something up to the value of eighteen thousand pounds."

"Sixteen," suggested Hamish. "And preferably second-hand."

"And the timing?" asked Isabel. "They haven't given us much time."

"I've been thinking about that," said Gordon. "He's only going for a test drive. He can't do the deal until the funds are assured. So perhaps we needn't worry too much about that."

Isabel rose to leave. Gordon looked at his watch. "A glass of sherry?" he asked.

Isabel demurred. "But don't let me inhibit

you," she said. "If you had some ordinary soda water, though, that would do me fine."

"Soda water?" said Gordon brightly. "Now, we can always do that—as it happens."

Hamish left the room and returned with a bottle of sherry and an old-fashioned soda-water syphon on a tray. He passed a glass of unadulterated soda water to Isabel. Then, having poured a small quantity of sherry into the two remaining glasses, he added a good splash of soda to each.

"I suppose we should toast the health of Cat and Leo," said Isabel. She realised she sounded grudging, and tried to make amends by smiling brightly.

They raised their glasses.

"Soda water is so refreshing," she said.

"My wife bought me this syphon for my birthday," said Gordon. "A long time ago. I brought it into the office and it's never really left the firm."

Soda water triggered a memory in Isabel's mind. "Do you know," she began, "that the Parsis have a lot of occupational surnames?"

Gordon looked blank. Hamish frowned in puzzlement.

"The Parsis were originally Persian," said Isabel. "They're still prominent in Mumbai. Successful business types. Accountants. Hoteliers. And they have these lovely surnames: they add **walla** to things."

"I know that word," said Gordon. "Isn't a **walla** an expert of some sort?"

"Yes," said Isabel. "So there are families called Bakerywalla—they must have been bakery people. And then there's Electricwalla."

"At least we know what they did," observed Hamish.

"But," said Isabel, "the Parsi surname to beat all others is Sodawaterwalla."

Hamish and Gordon both burst out laughing.

"Could I change my name?" asked Gordon. "I much prefer Gordon Sodawaterwalla."

"And you, Miss Philosophywalla?" said Hamish.

They laughed again, and Isabel left the office with a smile on her face. She would be quite happy to be Miss Philosophywalla, and Jamie, she decided, would obviously be Jamie Bassoonwalla.

She thought of Cat—Ms. Deliwalla. And

then she thought of Leo, Mr. Porscheturbowalla, and she stopped smiling. If her suspicion proved correct, Cat was about to make a serious mistake. Should she, as her aunt, not to mention her trustee, try to prevent the marriage? Surely Cat could see that if Leo was asking for a Porsche at this stage, there would be further requests, and these might not be so easily refused. Perhaps she should throw caution to the wind and say to Cat, "Look, Cat, this man is after your money. It's plain to see. He's starting with a Porsche. Stand by for more."

SHE WAITED until just before dinner to tell Jamie about the meeting with Hamish and Gordon, and the bombshell news about the Porsche. They had both been occupied with putting the boys to bed, and now, with the floor above in silence, they were able to catch up with one another in the kitchen. It was Jamie's turn to cook and he had proposed a cheese soufflé with an elaborate Lebanese salad. "Your man, Ottolenghi," said Jamie, arranging the salad ingredients in a line along the kitchen table. "He's not simple. Look at what he wants here: rose water, preserved lemon, marinated olives."

Isabel poured them both a glass of Chablis.

"I think I'd like to move to France," she said. "Or New Zealand, maybe. Anywhere where they make nice white wine like this. A small house at the edge of a village—if it's France. If it's New Zealand, a cottage on Golden Bay, maybe, or Marlborough Sound. Somewhere we could watch whales from the veranda."

Jamie busied himself with a jar of olives. "Houses in New Zealand are very small," he said. "They have low ceilings and not very big rooms."

"Does that matter?"

"Maybe; maybe not. I feel uncomfortable in a room with a low ceiling, though. I feel it's pressing down on me."

Isabel asked why he thought New Zealand houses were so small. Jamie thought for a moment. "They're modest people. They don't make a fuss."

"Quiet?"

At nineteen, Jamie had spent part of a gap year in New Zealand, teaching music at a boys'

school in Auckland. He hesitated before an-
swering. "For the most part, yes. They don't go
in for shouting. They like small-scale things."
He smiled as he remembered. "I was meant to
teach music, you know, but they tried to get
me to teach rugby instead. They were far more
interested in rugby than in music. They said
that since I came from Scotland, I must know
how to play rugby."

"And?"

"And I was very obliging at that age. I said,
'Sure, I'll teach rugby—if that's what you want
me to do.' So, they put me in charge of one
of their teams for really young players. These
boys were about eight—at the most. I did my
best, but the problem was that I didn't really
know the rules and so I made them up."

Isabel raised an eyebrow. "Made them **up**?
Invented them?"

Jamie nodded. "It would have been fine if
they hadn't arranged a game against another
of these boys' schools. I was to be the referee."

Isabel laughed. "I'm not sure if I want to
hear the end of this story."

"Neither do I," said Jamie. "But here goes,
anyway. I started to run the game according to

the rules I'd invented, but there were a whole lot of parents from the other school who had come along to watch. They couldn't believe what they were seeing. Their sons complained, and one or two fights broke out amongst the boys. That was the end of my career as a rugby teacher."

"Brief and distinguished," said Isabel.

"Anyway, why do you want to go to France or New Zealand? What's happened?"

She told him, and when she had finished he left the salad and sat down opposite Isabel at the kitchen table. "A Porsche **Turbo**?" he asked.

"Yes."

Jamie put his hands to his head. "Oh my God," he said. "That's it then."

Isabel waited.

"He's after her money."

Isabel nodded dumbly. "One likes to give people the benefit of the doubt."

"Isabel," said Jamie, "there **is** no doubt. He's getting her to buy him a Porsche Turbo. He's been fairly quick off the mark—one has to give him that." He paused. "It's a sort of fraud, really. He's getting this car from the trust. He's attempting to deceive them."

There was nothing Isabel could say to disagree with this. "I suppose I'm going to have to tell her outright."

"That the trust won't play ball?"

"Yes."

"Quite right," said Jamie. "And then tell him to his face—so that the message isn't watered down. Tell him, so he knows we're on to him."

Isabel knew what Cat's reaction would be. She was not an easy person to persuade about anything, and now that she had made up her mind there would be no changing it. And if there were to be a showdown over Leo, there was no doubt in Isabel's mind as to which way that would end. And predictably so: people who had to choose between family and a spouse or partner almost always chose the latter. She would do the same, she thought; if she had to choose between Jamie and an alternative, she would choose Jamie. Of course, Jamie was not Leo; in fact, he was very much the opposite, unless there were subtleties to

Leo that had so far escaped her. She did not think there were. A man who yearned for Porsche Turbos was . . . well, the sort of man who yearns for Porsche Turbos. There was no better way of putting it, dismissive though that sounded—condescending, even. She swallowed. She felt miserable.

Jamie put an arm about her. "Let me do it," he said.

She put her hand on his. "It's not your problem."

"It is," he said. "We share our problems—fifty-fifty. Remember words to that effect when Iain Torrance married us in the Canongate? Remember? Didn't he say something about worldly goods and so on? Worldly goods include problems—no doubt about that."

"She'll fly off the handle," said Isabel. "You know what she's like."

"I can cope with that," said Jamie. He glanced at the dinner ingredients. "I'd better cook supper."

She sat and watched him. How could I possibly deserve him? she asked herself. How had this happened? If one believed in reincarnation, of course, there would be an obvious explanation. In some previous life—presumably the last—she would have done some work of exceptional merit; some act of supererogatory generosity. She might have endowed a temple, perhaps, or helped some holy man in his journey, or just been generally kind. And this would all have been tallied up and her fate dictated: **Good husband next time.**

The great merit in such systems of belief was that they encouraged good behaviour, just as did our old beliefs in purgatory and hell. The problem, though, was that they were systems of belief that required a credulousness increasingly difficult to sustain. It was too late, Isabel thought, to be innocent.

Do I believe in God? she asked herself. She hated being asked that question by others but was just as uncomfortable asking it of herself. The problem was that sometimes she said yes, and sometimes no. Or answered evasively, in a way that enabled her to continue to believe in spirituality and its importance, and kept her from the soulless desert of atheism. For that, she thought, is what it was; and why should one not believe in something that may not be true, if it made life more bearable, did not make others cry, and gave us a reason to love those whom we needed to love?

The salad was delicious, but the soufflé collapsed before their eyes—like a discredited theory, Isabel thought—the moment Jamie placed it on the table. He was apologetic. "I followed the recipe to the letter," he protested. "And now look . . ."

She smiled at him. "It still tastes good," she said, and thought of "My Funny Valentine" that they had sung together the other night. Perhaps she should suggest some new words:

> **Do your soufflés end up flat**
> **On the plates where they are sat?**
> **Are they always underdone,**
> **Though making them is fun,**
> **Is it not?**
> **But don't change the recipe,**
> **Not if you care for me . . .**

He was looking at her. "Why are you smiling, Isabel?"

"I'm thinking about 'My Funny Valentine'— I've thought of some new lyrics."

She sang them to him. He smiled broadly. "Lovely," he said, and blew her a kiss. "And they'll be even better when sung in tune."

"You're the musician," she said. "I'm the philosopher."

"Perfect," he agreed. "What we call . . ."

"Harmony," she said.

CHAPTER SEVEN

BECAUSE JAMIE had promised to speak
to Cat that day, and because Grace had asked
if she might take the boys to the museum
after their nursery and playgroup, Isabel had
a whole day at her disposal. She decided that
she would work on the **Review,** with a view
to lowering, if not completely flattening, the
accusatory piles in her in-trays, real and meta-
phorical. That would mean she would be able
to go to the opening at the Scottish Gallery
that evening without a feeling of having to
be elsewhere and doing something else. She
would meet Jamie at the opening, and would
find out then the outcome of his meeting
with Cat. Or confrontation, rather—because

Isabel could not imagine it being anything else but that.

She wondered whether she should have allowed Jamie to do this. Messengers were always in peril of being shot, and Jamie would know that. Yet in this case, there was an additional danger that old business between the two of them might complicate matters. Jamie had once been Cat's boyfriend, even if the affair had lasted only a few months before Cat had broken it off. Isabel had been dismayed at that, as she felt that of all Cat's boyfriends—and there had been quite a number—Jamie stood out head and shoulders above the rest. Isabel had liked none of the others, try as she might. One or two she had actively disliked—such as Toby, the young man given to wearing crushed-strawberry cord trousers, and expressing strong views on just about every conceivable topic. Jamie had been the opposite of Toby, and when he was dismissed by Cat, Isabel had continued their friendship.

The relationship had changed, in spite of the fourteen years that separated them. The change from being a friend to being a lover is often not a simple one; in this case it was fraught with the additional complication of Cat's antipathy to the whole idea. In her eyes, although she never said it, there was something vaguely indecent about an aunt—even an aunt not all that much older than the niece—taking up with a discarded boyfriend. She had registered her disapproval through icy silences, should Jamie's name be mentioned, and through a hundred other small ways in which one person may make another person feel bad. This **froideur** had eventually thawed, but when Isabel became pregnant, it had returned—a more complex feeling now, combining envy, a sense of injustice, and annoyance that Isabel's life should seem to be going so well when her own life was not. Isabel knew that there was very little one could do about that feeling, other than to find the German word for it, which was **Gluckschmerz**—pain in the success or pleasure of another, the opposite of that equally useful term **Schadenfreude.**

Their relationship had been easier more recently, which was a matter of relief, but the engagement to Leo, and the transparently dishonest request that had followed, now threatened to set things back. The thought depressed her, and by the time she arrived at the Scottish Gallery for the opening she was prepared for the bleakest of reports from Jamie.

He was already there when she arrived. She saw him standing in an alcove, looking at a painting with Tommy Zyw, one of the gallery's directors. Tommy smiled, and beckoned for Isabel to join them. She liked Tommy, who was a keen and adventurous snow-boarder, and she always quizzed him as to the latest risks he had been taking.

Jamie gave her a welcoming kiss on the cheek, while Tommy fetched her a glass of wine.

"I have to know," she said. "I wanted to phone you, but I wasn't quite sure when you were going to be in rehearsal."

His demeanour was not what she had expected.

"Did you see her?" she asked.

He nodded. "It went very well."

It took Isabel a moment to deal with this. "You mean . . . You mean there wasn't a great scene?"

"That's right. Sweetness and light. No problem. **Hakuna matata,** so to speak."

Isabel gasped. "What happened?"

Tommy returned with Isabel's glass of wine, and they had to shelve the subject. Tommy enquired whether they knew the artist, and Isabel replied that they did not. They received invitations to all the openings at the gallery, and many of the artists were new to her. She did not explain that they were there that evening at the behest of Iain Melrose.

Tommy began to say something about the painting they were standing in front of, but was called away by one of the staff to deal with an enquiry. Isabel turned immediately to Jamie. "How come?" she asked. "Has Cat had an epiphany?"

Jamie shrugged. "Who knows? But it was a walk in the park compared with what I was expecting."

Isabel shook her head incredulously. "I'm astonished—I really am."

"I was too," said Jamie. "I called in at the deli and spoke to her in her office. I had a great welcome. She flashed her engagement ring all over the place and said that she was tremendously pleased to have found the very best man she had ever met. She repeated that. The very best man she had ever met. That was all before I had the chance to say anything—even congratulations."

Isabel giggled. "Obviously designed to put **you** in your place."

Jamie smiled. "I wouldn't want to be pushy." He took a sip of his wine and leaned forward to examine the painting more closely.

"Come on, Jamie," Isabel urged. "And then?"

He turned to face her. "I took the bull by the horns. I said that I had seen a letter on the table setting out the trustees' decision: no Porsche."

Isabel frowned. "I know it's an old-fashioned position—ludicrous, even—to disapprove of lying, but did you have to . . ."

"It just came to me," said Jamie. "And lies that just come to you aren't necessarily lies."

"Nonsense," said Isabel.

Jamie defended himself. "Well, what would you have me say? Should I have said: Isabel can't face giving you this news, but your application for a Porsche has been turned down?"

Isabel looked away. He was right, and she

now regretted accepting his offer to break the news to Cat. She should have done it herself, which was the more courageous thing to do. Now she should apologise to him—not only for criticising the stratagem to which he had resorted, but also for having allowed him to become involved in the first place.

"I'm sorry," she said. "It's just that I've been a bit jumpy about this. You know I don't find it all that easy to handle Cat."

He took her hand. "Of course you don't. Nobody does. Our friend Leo is going to find the same thing, I suspect."

"Do you think he knows that?"

Jamie was unsure. "I don't think he's the touchiest-feeliest character. I'm not sure if he thinks too much about emotions and the rest."

Isabel sighed. "I still see him as a . . . well, as a lion—a sort of half human, half lion. A chimaera, I suppose we'd call it. I know that's absurd, but that's the effect he has on me. That great mane of hair—and that's definitely lion-coloured; tawny."

"Yes, I suppose it is. Have you looked at its consistency?"

"No. Should I?"

Jamie rubbed a thumb and index finger together. "I wanted to feel it when I was talking to him. But you can't really do that, can you? You can't suddenly say, 'Do you mind if I **feel** your hair?'"

"You certainly can't," said Isabel.

"It's rough. It looks thicker than ordinary human hair."

Isabel raised an eyebrow. "Perhaps that's what she likes. A bit of texture." She paused, looking around to see if they could be overheard. Everybody was otherwise occupied, and a few of the guests were even looking at the pictures.

"It's his face too," Isabel continued, "and . . ." She dropped her voice even lower. "And his hands—the palms of his hands. They look as if they're padded. It's most peculiar, but they look like the pads of feline feet. Rough pads, just like a cat's."

Jamie's face broke into a grin. "Let's not fantasise too much."

"Oh, I know," said Isabel. "And yet it's what I pick up from him. It's a sense of being in the presence of another species." She paused. "Perhaps Cat is a sort of Circe. Do you think she might be?"

Jamie looked blank. "Circe?"

"The Odyssey?" Isabel prompted.

"Oh, her. The woman who changed people into animals?"

"Yes. She transformed Odysseus's men into pigs. But she had potions to change people in other ways. I saw a painting here—Tommy may remember it—of a man given the head of a lion by Circe. It's one of the saddest pictures I know. It made me feel—"

Jamie interrupted her. "Do you want to hear what happened?"

Isabel said she was sorry. "I know I have a tangent problem, but some tangents are just so interesting, I can't help going off along them."

"I like your tangents," said Jamie, fondly. "I wouldn't want it otherwise. But to get back to where we were, Cat was completely cool about the information. She just said, 'Oh, I didn't think they'd approve—but I thought I'd try.'" Jamie paused. "And so I said, 'You don't mind?' And she didn't hesitate; straightaway she said, 'I don't mind at all. It wasn't for the business, strictly speaking—it was for me. I'm fed up with my VW Golf.'"

Isabel's jaw dropped. She had not anticipated so brazen an explanation.

Jamie continued, "Then she said, 'They're sitting on stacks of cash. I don't see why I shouldn't have a bit of it.' So I said, 'I thought that perhaps Leo was behind the Porsche idea.'"

Isabel waited. Once again, the next disclosure was a surprise.

"I wondered whether she would resent my inference, but no, she didn't mind it at all. The true position, she said, was the exact opposite. 'Leo doesn't like those cars— Porsches, Lamborghinis and so on. He likes Land Rovers—and the older the better. He'd like to get his hands on a 1948 Defender, if he could—that's when they first started to make them.'

"I listened to this," Jamie continued, "with my eyes out on stalks. And to underline the message—if she was trying to give me a message—she said that Leo didn't even know about it."

Jamie stopped. He looked at Isabel, waiting

for her reaction. "I wasn't sure whether to believe her," he said. "But I do, you know. Having thought about it, I think that she was being completely truthful. I don't think this is anything to do with Leo—I really don't. What about you?"

Lost in thought, Isabel did not reply immediately. In her mind, she went over the possibilities. Cat was lying—that was one: they had tried something that had simply failed, and in order to protect her pride, she was affecting indifference. That was certainly possible. Then there was the possibility that she was telling the truth, for the reasons she had set out to Jamie. Who wouldn't be tempted to ask for something expensive if he or she thought there was a chance that the request would be granted? And then there was a third possibility, and that, as she thought about it, seemed all the more likely the more she considered it.

When you start negotiating for something, it is often a good strategy to ask for too much. Then, when your request is turned down, you come up with another one that is considerably more modest. **You didn't give me that, but**

**it would be churlish, surely, not to grant
me this more modest request.** It was a tried
and trusted bargaining technique of the sort
solemnly and interminably discussed in the
pages of airport books on negotiation and
management. This was what anxious execu-
tives, hoping to make their way up the cor-
porate ladder, read on their way to meetings.
And there, on the back cover, would be the
author's photograph, with a rehearsed smile
and all the confidence about him of one who
knows how to get what he wants.

She ran this possibility past Jamie, who
umm-ed and **ah**-ed before eventually saying,
"Let's see."

Tommy had returned. "Iain Melrose would
like to introduce you to the artist," he said.
"He's over there."

They followed Tommy to a small knot
of people standing on the edge of the main
display. Iain Melrose, seeing them approach,
made a beckoning gesture, and then leaned
over towards a tall, slightly emaciated man in
a brown Harris tweed jacket. This man turned
round and smiled in their direction, moving
slightly to open the circle to them.

"My cousin Jack," said Iain. "And Hilary, his wife."

A petite woman in a blue cocktail dress reached out to shake Isabel's hand.

"We've met," said Hilary.

Isabel was momentarily flustered. "Of course . . ."

"You won't remember," said Hilary. "Six years ago. Jury service."

Isabel's potential embarrassment evaporated. "Of course. The High Court. Yes, of course." And she did remember now, because they had spent three days in one another's company, along with the thirteen others who made up a Scottish jury of fifteen. She would never have made that connection without being prompted, but now it came back to her.

Jack turned to his wife. "Remember, Hill, you can't talk about those things. What happens in the jury room stays in the jury room."

"Oh, I know that," said Hilary. "And I've forgotten just about everything that was said."

Isabel was quick to agree. "Me too," she said. But she had not forgotten, now that the memory had been stirred.

Jack turned to Isabel. "It's good of you to

come tonight. It's an artist's nightmare that a show will open to an empty room."

Jamie said, "There's no danger of that with your work." Then he added, "I really like these paintings."

Hilary said, "Jack's style is maturing. That's what the **Guardian** critic said."

"She was twenty-two," said Jack, laughing.

"And Duncan Macmillan has been very complimentary," Tommy observed from the edge of the circle. "He's been writing about Jack for some years now. He says that he's the heir to Bonnard and Vuillard."

This seemed to embarrass Jack, who shook his head vigorously. "That's very kind of him," he said. "But I'm not fit to look at the dust from their chariot wheels as they drive past."

"I can see why Duncan would say that," observed Tommy. "Somebody else made a similar point. It's the intimate nature of what you paint."

Hilary, sensing her husband's discomfort, tactfully broke up the circle. Taking Isabel by the arm, she led her towards the window that looked out over the rear garden of the gallery.

"Iain told us about you," she said. "He

mentioned that you'd agreed to be the trustee of his will."

Isabel gripped the stem of her wineglass. This could be excruciating, she thought; I should not have accepted.

"He asked me rather out of the blue," she said, trying to sound casual. "I don't really know Iain."

Hilary seemed interested in this. "Really? I thought that perhaps you were an old friend."

"Not at all," said Isabel. "We have some connections, I suppose you might call them. He knew my father, who was a lawyer here in Edinburgh. But they did not know one another terribly well. And we have a mutual friend in Guy Peploe." She looked around the crowded gallery behind them, as if hoping for rescue by Guy. "He's over there."

Hilary glanced in the direction in which Isabel was looking. "Yes, of course. Guy has always been very supportive of Jack's work. All the way through. Years ago, he took some of his paintings down to the London Art Fair and I think that's what really got him started—at least with collectors down in England. He always had his followers here in Scotland."

"Jack's obviously doing well," said Isabel. "It must be terrible to have to struggle as an artist. You may know that your work's good, but the public doesn't always get it, does it?"

Hilary laughed. "Not to mention the critics." She looked out of the window. Isabel noticed that a thin stroke of eyeliner applied above her right eye had begun to run. She was lightly made up, her skin seeming supple. What age was she? Very early forties, thought Isabel—a few years younger than Jack. She had the air of somebody who went to the gym reasonably often, Isabel thought; or played tennis, as her upper arms were firm, even slightly muscular.

Hilary brought the conversation back to Iain. "It's very sad about Iain, isn't it? He looks so well, even now."

"He's being very brave, I imagine," said Isabel. "But so many people are, aren't they? They make the most of what time is left."

"Which I suppose is what we all should do," Hilary said, bringing her gaze back to Isabel. "We should all make the most of our time, because it's all finite, although in different measure."

Isabel wondered whether she should say **carpe diem.** It expressed everything that needed to be said on that subject, and expressed it rather succinctly, as Latin expressions tended to do. But Hilary continued, "I hope you don't mind my talking to you."

"Of course I don't," said Isabel. She would prefer not to be having this conversation, but that was not the same as minding talking to Hilary.

"You see," Hilary went on, "I wouldn't want you to think I was trying to influence any decision you might make."

Isabel took a deep breath. That was the fundamental problem with this arrangement: it was inevitable that when she met the potential beneficiaries they would try to make their case—it would be strange if they did not. After all, this was what in commercial circles was called a "beauty parade," where firms pitching for business sought to impress those who might give them a contract. "I think it's a rather odd situation, quite frankly. It's embarrassing for everybody." She paused. She would be scrupulously correct. If you played strictly according to the rules of the book, then you would have no reason to reproach yourself. If there **was** a book, of course.

"I have a completely open mind," she said. "Sorry if that sounds a bit pompous, but I think I should spell it out. I'll look at the basic question, which is: Who would be the most appropriate person to look after this estate that Iain is so fond of? And that will obviously involve hearing people's ideas for what might be done with it."

Hilary nodded her agreement. "Yes, precisely," she said. She lowered her voice. "But there's one thing I'd like to say right at the outset. Jack and I don't need the money. We're very comfortable."

"I thought that would be the case," said Isabel. "These paintings are flying off the wall." She had seen the exhibition price list: there was nothing under twenty thousand pounds, and one or two of the larger paintings were over sixty thousand.

"So Jack is not exactly the struggling artist."

"A nice position to be in," said Isabel, neutrally.

"The point I'm making," Hilary said, "is that we're completely relaxed about this. In fact, I think we'd both take the view that were we to be given the estate, we'd look upon it as an obligation, rather than an asset."

Isabel felt that she was being led to a conclusion. "You're saying you wouldn't sell it."

"That's exactly what I'm saying." She paused. "And, frankly, if it were up to me, I'd have nothing to do with it at all. Jack's different, though: he has a very strong sense of duty."

It seemed that this was the note on which Hilary wanted the conversation to end. Taking Isabel's forearm, she led her gently towards a large painting around which the crowd had thinned. "Will you come and see us?" she asked. "Some time in the next few days?"

Isabel nodded. "If I may. I haven't really had the chance to chat to Jack very much."

"An opening is the very last occasion to try to engage with an artist," said Hilary. "May I call you to arrange things? You might like to see Jack's studio. We're in the Grange—not far from your friends Peter and Suzie Stevenson."

"I'd like it very much," said Isabel. She was puzzled: How did Hilary know that she was friendly with the Stevensons? Was Edinburgh **that** village-like? she asked herself.

She gave Hilary her number and then turned to look at the painting.

"You see the man's hands," said Hilary, pointing at the picture. "See how strong they are."

"Yes," said Isabel.

"He does hands very well," said Hilary. "Better than anybody, I'd say—other than Bonnard."

Jamie arrived at Isabel's side. Isabel noticed that when he came to stand beside her, Hilary gave him an appreciative glance. It was what virtually all women did when they saw him, and Isabel was used to it; she was usually bemused by it—rarely was she resentful.

"My husband," said Isabel.

Hilary recovered herself quickly. Her look, just a few seconds ago, thought Isabel, had been unmistakeably carnal. Women, thought Isabel, by and large did not mentally undress men in the way in which many men mentally undressed women, but some did. Hilary was one of them.

Jamie said, "I think it's getting on."

Isabel glanced at her watch. She was keen, now, to get away. "So it is," she said.

She turned to Hilary. "Would you mind if we slipped away? We have something else on."

"Of course not," said Hilary. "And these occasions get a bit warm, don't they?"

They said goodbye and made their way towards the front door. Isabel had something she needed to confide to Jamie—something troubling that she thought had just made this self-imposed task of hers markedly more difficult. She would talk to him about it later, once she had had the opportunity to reflect.

CHAPTER EIGHT

Every tuesday, the Institute of Advanced Studies in the Humanities had its fellows' lunch. This was something of a picnic, to which people brought fruit and sandwiches which they ate while listening to a work-in-progress paper by a visiting scholar. Isabel was an anonymous supporter of the institute, signing a generous cheque twice a year to support its activities, and in return was invited to its functions. She was an occasional participant in the Tuesday lunch, choosing to listen to various obscure and recondite papers on subjects she might otherwise never have explored. In recent months she had enjoyed listening to a visiting Italian

professor on the roots of **commedia dell'arte,**
an English social historian on self-help societ-
ies in nineteenth-century pottery towns and,
inadvertently, Professor Robert Lettuce on the
ethics of memory.

Professor Lettuce had been a substitute for
a speaker who had been afflicted with a heavy
cold and had called off at the last moment.
Isabel had been surprised to see him there when
she arrived, and even more surprised when she
learned that he was that afternoon's speaker.
For his part, Lettuce had been courteous, although distant. He still resented Isabel's ownership of the **Review,** which he had previously
tried to take over for his own purposes. He had
other grounds for resentment, one of which
was his suspicion that Isabel was somehow
a threat to his ambitions within philosophical circles in Edinburgh. This she was not: if
Professor Lettuce felt thwarted in Edinburgh,
it was because of his failure to understand
that he was in Scotland, a nation with its own
traditions and preoccupations. That was not
always fully appreciated by academics whose
focus was Oxbridge or London.

Now, as she entered the room in which

the Tuesday lunchtime seminars took place, Isabel saw that there was no sign of Lettuce. She recognised one or two of the members of staff from his department, along with the director and administrator of the institute. Finding a seat in the back row, she unwrapped the salad roll she had brought for her picnic and picked up her copy of the information sheet that had been placed on each seat. **Professor George van Driem, she read, is Professor at the University of Bern and will be talking today on the classification of Himalayan languages.**

Professor George van Driem . . . The name was vaguely familiar, but Isabel could not immediately recall where she had heard it. She looked towards the front of the room where a tall, distinguished-looking man was conferring with the director of the institute. Her gaze moved over the heads of the audience, now rather larger than the normal crowd expected at the Tuesday lunch. And that was when she saw Hamish and Gordon sitting only a couple of rows away from her, Hamish eating a sandwich and Gordon peeling an orange. Hamish turned at almost the moment

Isabel saw him, and nudged Gordon to alert him to Isabel's presence.

It came back to Isabel. Hamish and Gordon's conversation could have a stream of consciousness tone to it, but it had its saliences: now she remembered their mentioning a Dutch professor they had met in Nepal. That would explain their presence at the seminar.

The chairs next to Isabel being unoccupied, the two lawyers now came across to join her.

"Do you mind?" Hamish asked. "I couldn't believe it when I saw you—I know nobody here, not a soul."

"It's not our usual milieu," said Gordon. "Mary and I go to the lectures at the National Gallery, but that's about it." Mary was Gordon's wife, a rather worried-looking woman with an interest in horses, who was related, in some unspecified way, to the inventor of the telephone.

"I suppose this is pretty much your turf," said Hamish. "But when George got in touch to say he was giving a lecture in Edinburgh, we had to be here. We met him in Nepal, you see, when we were on the country-dancing trip."

"Yes," said Isabel. "I remember your telling

me." How could one forget? she asked herself, and she smiled at the thought of the two lawyers and their group of similarly minded friends, all bekilted, performing their dances in those unlikely and remote locations. The world was a strange and varied place, she reminded herself, and the odd things that people did in it should not surprise us.

It seemed that the lecture was about to begin, as the director was now showing George to a seat on a small, slightly raised podium at the front of the room.

"By the way," whispered Hamish. "I gather you spoke to Cat about . . ." He made a vague movement with his right hand, suggestive of complication.

"Yes," replied Isabel. "Or rather, Jamie did. I was going to have a word with her, but he did it."

Hamish looked at her enquiringly. "And?"

"It went very smoothly, apparently. She said that it was her idea and that she thought she'd just give it a try."

Hamish's face registered his surprise. "Well! I hadn't anticipated that."

"Nor had I. So, it seems there's no problem."

Hamish dusted a few crumbs of his sandwich off his trouser leg. "Maybe. Maybe not. Because . . ." He paused. On the podium, the director had turned to face the audience.

"Well, everybody," he said, "regulars and visitors: I hope you've enjoyed your lunches. Since you brought them with you, that is a matter for yourselves, of course."

There was a polite ripple of laughter.

Hamish leaned towards Isabel. "Because we received this morning another application to the trust from Cat. This time for a Land Rover."

Isabel caught her breath. "A Land Rover?" she whispered back.

"Yes, a Land Rover."

"Oh," she said. But that was all, as George van Driem had stood up now and had started his lecture on the classification of the Himalayan languages.

"Where do the Himalayan languages come from?" he asked. "Is this an important question? Very, I would say. Very."

Isabel listened. It was an engaging talk, and over the hour that followed, she was caught up in the complex issue of how the languages of the Himalayas are classified. But even as Professor van Driem spoke, from time to time she found her mind straying to thoughts of Land Rovers. Jamie had reported Cat's claim that Leo had had nothing to do with the Porsche, and that what he was really interested in was Land Rovers. And now they had an application for a Land Rover; ostensibly, no doubt, for use in the deli business.

Isabel fumed. Did Cat think she was so naïve as to not be able to work out what was going on? If Cat did think that, then she would have to be disabused of the notion. Isabel reached this conclusion reluctantly; after Jamie's conversation with Cat, she had thought confrontation had been side-stepped. It appeared that this was not the case. It would not be so easy to reject a request for a Land Rover, a more practical and appropriate working vehicle than a Porsche. Should they simply accede to this request—which would be the least troublesome course of action—or should they stand up to Cat and say that they thought it was really an attempt by Leo to get his hands on something at somebody else's expense?

She listened to Professor van Driem and to what he had to say about the Himalayan languages. She stared at the map he revealed on the board behind him, with its wavering boundary lines snaking vast swathes of high Himalaya. She followed his account of the manipulation of linguistic evidence for political purposes: languages and states were sometimes coterminous, and sometimes not. Behind languages there might be empires and armies. She looked out of the window behind the speaker: the sky was clear; there were birds in a nearby tree, and they sang. She thought: Why do there have to be such layers of complication behind the simplest of our human activities? She thought of Brother Fox, who slipped through her garden at night, sometimes spotted, sometimes unseen, and of the apparent simplicity of his existence, which would not really be simple at all, even without language to complicate it. Was that the problem? Had language changed everything for us—so irredeemably that it would prove to be humanity's downfall? Had we remained largely dumb, occupying a world of only a few sounds, as most animals do, would it have been easier for our bruised and battered world? Undoubtedly. Undoubtedly. She looked at Hamish, who was staring at the floor, concentrating on the Himalayan languages, clearly concerned by what he was hearing. She looked at Gordon, who was trying to extract a piece of orange pith from his teeth. She made her decision. She would tell Hamish and Gordon to agree to the Land Rover. Now was not the time for a battle: Cat would have to learn her hard lessons herself.

IT WAS ISABEL'S TURN to cook that evening, and she had decided on something straightforward: French onion soup followed by tuna steaks with salad. She knew that both of these were favourites of Jamie's, and they had the added attraction of being undemanding, and Isabel was in the mood for something simple. As she prepared the French onion soup, she told Jamie of the revelation that Hamish had sprung on her at the lunchtime lecture. When she mentioned the Land Rover request he buried his head in his hands. And when she went on to say that she had suggested to the lawyers that they approve the request, he raised both arms in a gesture of helpless resignation.

"That's complete capitulation," he said, his voice rising. "He's got away with it."

Isabel tried to reassure him. "It's just one thing—and she is entitled to help from the trust."

"He'll come back for more," said Jamie. "And Cat won't twig."

"We don't know that," said Isabel. "And anyway, I just couldn't face a big row right at the moment."

He waited for her to explain.

"I'm feeling the stress of that foolish under-taking of mine."

Jamie laughed. "Which foolish undertaking are you referring to?"

No sooner had he asked the question than he regretted it. Throughout their marriage, he had advised caution, trying to dissuade Isabel from too readily becoming involved in the problems of others. She knew of her failing in that respect, and had promised to do some-thing about it, but it never seemed to work. Her resolve not to get involved lasted until the next time an appeal was made for her help, and that was the point at which it faltered. It frustrated Jamie, but it also made him proud of her. He would not have liked to be married to a mean-spirited person, and Isabel was the walking antithesis of that.

So he blushed, and said, "I'm sorry, Isabel. I didn't mean that."

She hesitated, but then smiled; if there had been a barb, she chose not to notice it. She knew why he felt the way he did, and she, for her part, felt bad about that.

She reminded him of their meeting with Jack and Hilary the previous evening. "There was something worrying me," she said.

"I could tell there was," he said. "I sensed there was something."

"Yes, there was. I didn't want to bother you with it, but now . . ."

"You shouldn't worry about bothering me," he said quietly. "You know you can tell me anything—and vice versa."

"Of course."

He looked at her expectantly. "So?"

"I mentioned to you that I'd met her before—a long time ago."

"Yes, you did. It was on jury service, you said."

"Yes. We were both picked for jury service at the High Court. I was hoping they'd excuse me, on the grounds that I was self-employed, but they did not. So I found myself being sworn in, along with fourteen others, of whom Hilary was one. She looked a bit different then—longer hair, I think—which is probably why it took me a little while to recognise her yesterday."

"What was the case?" asked Jamie. "Anything interesting?"

"I think some people were hoping for a juicy murder, or something like that. Blackmail, I suppose, is always fun, but they were due for a disappointment. It was fraud. A very respectable businessman called Dougal Macglashian was charged with getting people to invest in dicey propositions. It was all to do with the wording of a company prospectus."

"Dry stuff," said Jamie.

Isabel agreed that it was, but pointed out that the consequences had been anything but dry for the people who'd taken the bait. "Some of them lost their life savings. One woman put in everything she owned and lost the lot. I particularly remember her. She had savings of about thirty thousand, I think. She was a hairdresser—a single mother whose son had cystic fibrosis. I don't know who put her in touch with this Macglashian—perhaps it was some useless financial adviser. Anyway, she lost every single penny. And this man sat in the dock, dressed in a smart suit, writing the evidence down on a yellow pad as if he were a court reporter. And it was all about him and his lies."

Jamie winced. "Horrible," he said. "Did you . . ." He left the question unfinished.

"Convict him? No, we didn't. I would have—and there were quite a few others like me. You have to get at least eight jurors to convict in Scots law. We had eight who wouldn't, and so he was found not guilty. That was that."

Jamie was silent. "So you were outvoted?"

Isabel nodded. "We're not meant to talk about it—even now. In fact, I haven't said anything about it to anybody—ever—except you."

"I think the law assumes you'll talk to your

spouse," said Jamie. "As long as you don't take it further than that."

"I doubt it, but I trust you."

He smiled. "That's nice to know." And then his smile faded. "That man . . . what happened to him?"

"He went back into business," said Isabel. "He had his own firm called something-or-other finance—I forget what it was. But he had an office not far from Charlotte Square—the lot. Brass plate and so on. You sometimes saw his photograph in the **Scotsman.** He was a big donor to charities. You read about him sponsoring Scottish yachts in these big international races. It was all high-profile stuff."

Jamie looked thoughtful. "Those people—the jurors—who thought he was innocent—why?"

Isabel had been peeling an onion. She put it down. "There's a poem about onions that I sometimes think about. It's Craig Raine, I think. He said that it's the onion memory that makes him cry." She looked at Jamie. "Don't you love that? You peel off a layer of memory and you find the tears well up."

He was silent, but eventually said, "You aren't crying because of the memory of that case?"

She shook her head. "No, this is physiological. It's all to do with something called syn-Propanethial S-oxide. It stimulates the tear glands. It's not a very poetic name, is it? 'It is the syn-Propanethial S-oxide that makes me cry' . . . doesn't quite work as poetry."

She put the knife under the tap and ran it for a moment. Then she turned to Jamie, and continued, "She was the one who turned most of them. It was Hilary. She argued very strongly that he was innocent."

"On what grounds?" asked Jamie.

"She claimed that she could always tell whether somebody was lying. She said she was one hundred per cent sure that Macglashian was telling the truth."

"She had no other grounds?"

"No," said Isabel. "But she was really persistent, and, I think, pretty convincing. There were quite a few people on that jury who had lost track of the proceedings more or less at the beginning. They simply didn't understand.

They were easily led, and I think they were swayed by the thought that if they acquitted him, they would at least not have to worry about convicting an innocent man."

"So that was that?"

Isabel nodded. "But there's something more—and this is what's been preying on my mind since yesterday. This is what I really need to talk to you about."

She resumed the chopping of the onion, dabbing once or twice at her eyes with the corner of a tea towel. "About six months later—or maybe a little more—I was in Bruntsfield one morning. I had been at Cat's and went over to the newsagent to pick up a paper. I dropped in at La Barantine for a coffee. I was sitting at one of those tables in the window when I saw them up at the counter, paying for their coffee and croissants, and about to leave. It was them—Hilary and Macglashian."

Jamie stared at her. "Definitely together?"

"Yes. Together. They were talking as the woman behind the counter fiddled with the credit card machine. I buried my nose in my paper—I did not want her to see me—and she didn't. But once they were outside, I was able to see them walk a short distance up the road. Her husband was there—in the street. They shook hands—it looked quite formal, but they were not strangers; they were friends, I would have thought."

Jamie considered this in silence.

"I didn't know what to think," said Isabel. "I spoke to a friend of mine who said that he thought there was no reason why a juror should not socialise with somebody who's been acquitted of an offence. He said that it was probably unwise, as it could suggest some sort of collusion between them, during the trial, but that was not necessarily the case."

Jamie thought about this. "It doesn't smell right," he said.

"No," said Isabel. "And I suppose there are times when we should trust our sense of smell."

Isabel finished scraping the sliced onion into a pot, poured some olive oil in, and put it on a ring of the cooker. There was a soft, sizzling sound. Neither of them spoke for a while. Then Jamie said, "This changes the way you feel about her?"

Isabel nodded. "It does. It means I don't trust her."

"I didn't warm to her," mused Jamie. "There was something about her that put me off."

"Pushiness?"

He hesitated. "There was a bit of that," he said. "But I'm not sure if it was just that. It was . . . a sort of creepiness. I can't think of any other word for it."

"And yet," said Isabel, "if one is making a choice on proper grounds—and that, after all, is why I've been asked to do this—then one can't rely on some sort of intuition."

"Well, I have an intuition that this woman is bad news," said Jamie.

Isabel moved the pot off the ring, and the sizzling subsided. "I'll take that into account," she said. She reached for a jar of rich beef stock and decanted it into the pot.

"Why do I like French onion soup so much?" asked Jamie.

"You ate it as a boy? For most of us, that's the reason we like things. Childhood exposure."

"The Jesuit claim?" said Jamie. "Didn't they say: give us a child until he's seven and we'll give you the man?"

"They stand accused of saying that," said Isabel.

Jamie laughed. "Give a boy French onion soup until he's seven, and he'll eat it for life."

"Possibly. But it can work the other way. I know somebody who can't eat pineapple because she was forced to have it as a child."

When the meal was ready, they sat down and ate for a while in silence before Isabel said, "I'm going to have to see this through, I suppose. I said I would."

Jamie did not try to dissuade her. "Do it quickly," he said. "Get the facts and then make a quick decision. Trust your intuitions."

She did not disagree, but thanked him—for everything.

"I'll play the piano for you after dinner," he said. "Nothing demanding."

"And sing?"

"Yes, we can sing."

" 'My Love's in Germany,' " Isabel suggested.

"If that'll help."

"It always does."

He looked at his plate. **"My love's in Germany,"** he muttered. **"Send him hame, send him hame! My love's in Germany—send** him hame! He's as brave as brave can be, he would rather fa' than flee, But his life's so dear to me—send him hame, send him hame!"

Isabel asked, "Can French onion soup make you cry?"

Jamie thought it unlikely.

"Then it's those words," said Isabel quietly.

CHAPTER NINE

SATURDAY was the busiest day at Cat's deli, and for this reason one on which Isabel often helped out. Jamie was off that weekend— he sometimes had rehearsals on a Saturday afternoon—and so he agreed to take the boys on an outing while Isabel worked at Cat's. Craigie's Farm, on the outskirts of Edinburgh, overlooking the Firth of Forth, was a favourite place of Charlie's, as there were old tractors, painted bright red and put out for children to clamber over, tolerant pigs to be prodded, and a restaurant that sold large slices of irresistible iced cake.

There was no sign of Cat when Isabel went

into the deli that morning at ten. Eddie explained that she had gone to meet her organic-egg supplier in East Lothian but would be back by eleven at the latest. In the meantime, if Isabel was prepared to slice peppers for marinating in olive oil, stuff large green olives with garlic, and, when she had finished that, make enough rice salad to see them through until Tuesday, then that would leave him free to deal with the customers. She agreed, and donned the gloves and apron that always made her feel a bit like a surgeon in an operating theatre. "A few germs would probably do people good," she remarked to Eddie, who smiled and said, "We can't have germs, Isabel. Not these days."

"Actually, Eddie," she replied, as she slipped the uncomfortable latex gloves over her fingers, "we're all covered in germs. You, me, Cat, even the Prime Minister. Everybody. And we need to be exposed to unfamiliar germs too, if our immune systems are to stay in good shape."

Eddie was not impressed. "Food's different," he said. "You mustn't let germs get on food."

"Some germs, yes. But others . . . if you

had no germs on food, then we'd all have al-
lergies and would end up being able to eat
hardly anything."

Eddie shrugged. "My cousin can't eat anything. He's allergic to milk and anything to
do with milk. And wheat too, I think. He
just eats chips and burgers without the rolls.
And Irn-Bru. He drinks four litres of Irn-Bru
a day."

Isabel winced. Irn-Bru was the most popular
of Scottish sugary drinks—a pale orange con-
coction tasting like liquid chewing gum, but an
established part of Scottish urban mythology.

"Anyway," Eddie continued, "anyway, here
he comes."

Isabel followed Eddie's gaze out of the window. A taxi had drawn up outside, and the
passenger emerging was Leo.

"She didn't say he was coming in," muttered Eddie. "And he never helps when he
comes here. He just sits and drinks coffee and
offers advice."

Isabel was uncertain what to do. She had
not seen Leo since the announcement of the
engagement, and she would have to invite the
two of them round to celebrate. It was already

going to seem a little late to do so; she could not put it off any longer. She began to peel off the gloves she had just put on.

Eddie frowned. "I thought you were going to do the peppers . . ."

"I shall," said Isabel. "But I need to have a quick chat with Leo. Sorry, Eddie—I won't be long."

"He's a waste of space," said Eddie. "A complete waste of space."

"Don't be too hard on him, Eddie," said Isabel. "We're going to have to live with him."

"Not me," Eddie muttered. "He's nothing to do with me."

Leo came into the deli. He did not close the door behind him, and this brought a loud "Do you mind closing the door?" from Eddie.

Leo smiled. "Born in a tent," he said, reaching behind him for the door handle. Noticing Isabel behind the counter, he waved cheerfully to her. "Isabel! I thought it was you."

"Who else would it be?" muttered Eddie **sotto voce.**

Isabel gave Eddie a discouraging glance and made her way out from behind the counter to greet Leo. He seemed pleased to see her, leaning forward to kiss her on both cheeks. Her natural reaction was to freeze, but with an effort she conquered that, giving his upper arm a quick, friendly squeeze.

"I'm so happy for you," she said. "For both of you, of course. It's very good news." How easily, she thought, come the untruths; how effortless the hypocrisy. And she thought, for a moment, of Immanuel Kant. And George Washington, for that matter, if we imagined that he really did say, "Father, I cannot tell a lie." How would a Kantian greet an unwelcome engagement? With silence?

She felt his lips on the skin of her cheek, a brief, slightly abrasive touch, complicated by stubble. She noticed that he had a smell about him that was really quite strong when close up—a dusty sort of smell; sandalwood and the smoke of a woodfire. It was not unpleasant, but it was nonetheless strange. It's the smell of lion, she suddenly thought. This was what a lion smelled like—a tawny smell, a smell of the dry bushveld. Absurd. Absurd. But she drew in the scent again and she saw the landscape from which it emanated: savanna, golden grass, acacia trees.

She drew back. "I'm sorry I wasn't in touch earlier. Jamie and I have been talking about having you both round to celebrate. We must arrange it."

He inclined his head in acknowledgement of the invitation. "That would be nice. Really nice. I'll bring the Prosecco."

Isabel smiled. "We might run to the real thing."

Leo looked across the counter. "Hear that, young Eddie? Real champagne. How about that?"

Eddie turned away in distaste, but Leo did not seem to notice.

Isabel suggested they sit down for a cup of coffee at one of the tables. Leo agreed, and she asked Eddie if he would mind making coffee for them. He looked at her, his upper lip quivering, and then, grudgingly, said that he would bring it over.

At the table, Isabel asked about their plans. "Is this going to be a long engagement?" she asked.

Leo laughed. "Do you mean: Is it going to last long?"

"No, of course I didn't mean that. I meant: When are you planning to get married?"

Leo shrugged his shoulders. "A month. Maybe two months from now."

"Fairly soon, then."

"Oh yes, as soon as we can get things sorted out. I don't know if Cat told you—we're going to buy a boat."

Cat had not said anything about a boat.

"I didn't know you sailed," said Isabel.

"Yes, I have my Yachtmaster's certificate. I want to do more of it in the future. So Cat and I have decided—we'll get rid of this place and buy a boat on the west coast. Oban or somewhere near there. There's a place at Port Appin that could suit us. We'd get a mooring."

Isabel struggled to take this in. "You mean you'll **live** on the boat? All the time?"

Leo nodded. "Yes. We'll live on her in the summer, while we take people out to the islands. We'll do skippered charters—you charter the yacht and the skipper, so you don't need to know how to sail. People like it."

Isabel still struggled. "A big boat, then?" she asked.

Leo made fun of her question. "A big boat? Yes, a big boat all right. Sixty-two feet— at least. Six cabins."

Isabel tried to envisage sixty-two feet. In her mind's eye she saw Leo, wearing frayed trousers, barefoot, climbing up a mast, his mane of leonine hair ruffled by the wind.

"And then in the winter," Leo went on, "we'll sail her over to the Caribbean to do the season there. Antigua. Saint Vincent. Those places."

Eddie came over with their coffee.

"That's the stuff, Eddie boy," said Leo, as Eddie put the cup before him. And then he added, "Fancy a job as a cabin boy?" He laughed. "Only joking."

Eddie glowered.

"Thank you, Eddie," said Isabel gently. Then, to Leo she said, "I didn't realise that Cat was keen on the sea."

"She is," said Leo. "She came over with me to look at a boat that's on the market over at Ardfern. It's a beauty. We're getting a marine surveyor to look at her early next week. He'll do a very thorough job."

Isabel took a sip of her coffee. It was too hot. "Oh yes?"

"Yes. He'll probably take a look at the engine oil to see if there's any evidence of metal fragments. That'll tell him a lot about the gearbox. And the hull—they go over that with a fine-tooth comb to look out for blistering. Osmosis. Damage that's been painted over. Not that this one should have much of that— she's only been in the water for two seasons."

"She sounds lovely," said Isabel.

"Expensive," said Leo. "But you know something, Isabel? You get what you pay for. If people only bore that in mind, they'd avoid a whole shovel-load of trouble, I'm telling you."

"Probably," said Isabel. She was wondering how expensive was expensive. She toyed with her coffee. "Do you mind my asking, how much do these things cost?"

"New?" asked Leo. "Or second-hand?"

"Well, new, I suppose."

"This is a Swedish boat," said Leo. "You'd pay about eight hundred thousand for it new. Second-hand . . ." He hesitated. "Half a million, if it's almost new. And this one is."

Isabel drew in her breath. "Half a million? That's rather a lot."

"But remember, you make money with charter fees."

"Even so," she said.

"Even so," he agreed. "But we'll sell this place, and Cat says that there's a trust that can help her with her business expenses. The boat will be a business asset, don't you think?"

Isabel did not reply. This was a major raid on the trust. Cat was entitled to support from the trust, but of course any money that went to Cat was, in a sense, money taken from the principal beneficiary—and that was Isabel. She wondered what would happen if Cat and Leo split up? Would the boat be in his name, or in Cat's? Or in both? If it were to be in Leo's name, then the purchase of the boat could be a very successful way of his effectively getting his hands on just about all of Cat's assets. And yet could she do anything about it? Or **should** she do anything about it? It was Cat's life, and Isabel could not lead it for her. If she wanted to entangle her finances with Leo's, then that was her prerogative, and Isabel should stand back. People had to learn for themselves; they had to be allowed to take risks and make mistakes.

"Well," prompted Leo. "What do you think? If they'd advance, say, one hundred grand, that would make all the difference. I've had this place valued, and we should get four hundred grand for it."

Isabel stared at the tablecloth. Cat's deli had been part of her life for some time now, and there was Eddie to think about too. What would happen to Eddie? He had never worked anywhere else, and it was clear to Isabel that the deli was his life.

"What about your own contribution?" Isabel asked. "Will you be putting anything into it?"

Leo grinned. Bending his arm, he pointed to his bulging biceps. "Muscle," he said. "That's what I bring to the party." He paused. "And planning, of course."

Isabel said nothing for a few moments. Then, looking over towards the counter, where Eddie was serving a customer, she said, her voice lowered, "Does Eddie know?"

Leo shook his head. "Not yet. We'll tell him. We're getting somebody round to prepare to market the business. We're ready to sell it as a going concern, but they've told us we may get more from somebody wanting to turn it into a full-scale coffee bar. There's not much margin on deli products, you know."

Isabel bit her lip. "He likes his job, you know. It's very important to him."

"Him?" Leo nodded curtly in Eddie's direction. "He'll get something else. He's a bit wet, but he should find something."

"Is your mind made up?" asked Isabel. "Is this definitely going to happen?"

Leo looked surprised that anybody would doubt him. "Yes, of course it is."

"Oh well," said Isabel, resignation in her voice. "You've given me a lot to think about."

Leo smiled. "You're a philosopher, aren't you? Isn't that what you like?"

AFTER THEY HAD FINISHED their coffee, Leo retreated to Cat's office, to wait for her there. "I have a whole stack of emails to deal with," he said. "Boat stuff mostly. I'll keep out of your way." Isabel returned to work, and by the time Cat returned from her visit to the egg supplier, she had replenished most of the cold prepared food that would be needed for their lunchtime customers. Eddie was largely silent, sulking over Leo's presence. Isabel glanced at him from time to time, but he turned away, avoiding contact. She wanted to talk to him, but she was not sure what to say. They could discuss Leo, and how important it was for Cat that this should work out, but now that Leo had revealed their plans to Isabel, any such discussion seemed a bit pointless. If the deli was going to be sold, as looked likely, then Eddie's job would become uncertain—at best. The purchaser, whoever it might be, could keep him on, perhaps, but in such circumstances he was just as likely to replace him. Eddie would not come across well in an interview. He was hard-working—Isabel knew that—but he liked to handle things his way and did not take well to being told what to do.

Cat was in a good mood when she arrived.

"Leo's in the office," Isabel told her. "We had coffee together."

Cat kissed Isabel warmly. "You're such a star, Isabel—you really are." Glancing at the refrigerated counter, she went on, "And look at what you've done. Everything's fantastic. You're a star."

Isabel wiped her hands on her apron. "Oh well," she said.

"Where are the boys?" asked Cat.

"With Jamie at Craigie's Farm. They love going there."

Cat nodded. "They have pigs, don't they? Jamie always said he liked pigs."

This surprised Isabel. Jamie had never said that to her. "Did he?" she asked, almost automatically.

"Oh yes. Has he never told you? He told me that he used to dream about pigs."

Isabel frowned. Why would anybody dream about pigs? Unless, of course, you kept pigs: if pigs were part of your daily life, then your dreams, she imagined, might revolve around pigs. But Jamie?

She looked at Cat. She wanted to talk to her about her conversation with Leo. If she and Leo were thinking of selling the deli, then she had a right to know about that. She had helped Cat with the business for some years now—entirely without pay—and that gave her a right, she felt, to be kept informed if there were to be any major plan for it. It was wrong of Cat—quite wrong—to keep her in the dark about something as fundamental as that: she had a right to know.

She began to feel resentment well up within her. This was what it must feel like to be a worker in a company whose future was being planned far above one's head. This was what it must be like to be a tiny, helpless part of a vast machine, knowing that you have no control over your very means of earning a living. You may have worked in a job for thirty years, given it your all, and the owner suddenly decides that you, and the job you have been doing, are no longer necessary. And that's it. Of course, Isabel knew that the analogy was far-fetched: she was not dependent on the deli; she was not even on the paid staff. If it were closed tomorrow, it would make not an iota of difference to her material situation. But Eddie was different. Eddie would be affected.

She could not contain herself. Drawing Cat aside, she whispered, "Leo told me about the boat."

Cat did not respond immediately, but

glanced over Isabel's shoulder towards Eddie, who was wrapping ham for a customer. Then she said, "I haven't told Eddie yet."

"I assumed so," said Isabel. "And you hadn't told me either."

Cat gave a start. "You? I was going to. We've only just decided."

"You might have kept me informed," said Isabel. "I . . . I . . ." She struggled to work out what she wanted to say. Then, "I resent it, you know. I really do. I help you as much as I can, Cat, and you'd think you'd at least let me know about something like this." She paused, before adding, "So it's definite then?"

Cat seemed unmoved by the reproach. "Yes. It's going on the market at the end of next week. There's an agent called Tom Something—I forget his other name. Leo knows him from the gym."

Isabel closed her eyes. She saw Leo in the gym, in a loincloth, swinging, like Tarzan, from a rope. She wanted to say, "Does Leo swing on ropes?" but she did not. Instead she said, "And does this Tom Something think there'll be buyers?"

"Oh, heaps," said Cat. "This is in a good

position, you see. As you know. In retail it's all about position. Ten yards can make the difference between success and bankruptcy. Footfall. That's what you need, footfall."

"Heaps of people will want to buy it as a deli?"

Cat shook her head. "Not necessarily. Apparently, Tom told Leo that he already has somebody interested who wants to make it into a hair salon. There's this guy called Jonny Mustique. No **h** in the Jonny, and Mustique as in the island. That's his business name, of course. He's probably really called Davey Macdonald, or something like that. He has four other salons in Edinburgh, and they all do pretty well. I think I may have met him, actually, at a wedding last year. He's friendly with Kirsty Dawes—remember her?—I was at school with her. She married that man from Perth—the one who had the gliding accident."

Isabel's irritation grew. "This Jonny Mustique—how serious is he?"

"Very, according to Tom. That's what Leo says, anyway."

Isabel took a deep breath. "And you don't mind if it stops being a deli?"

Cat seemed puzzled by this question. "Why should I mind what happens?"

Isabel looked at Cat despairingly. Where did one begin with somebody who had that attitude? Surely this was at the heart—the very heart—of how we treated the world. We minded what happened after us.

She decided to try. "People are often concerned about what happens to their businesses. They spend years building them up and so it's natural to want them to . . . to keep going, I suppose."

Cat looked uninterested. "What difference does it make?"

Isabel gritted her teeth. **Unaware privilege,** she thought. "It can make a big difference to some people."

"Which people?" Cat asked. "And why? Why should it matter if one business closes and another opens?"

Isabel felt her anger mounting. "People need a certain amount of stability in their lives," she said. "If people lose a local shop, they miss it. They may not be able to get what they need."

Cat made a careless gesture. "They can get things online."

"And there are jobs too. Online businesses don't create many jobs. And look at the conditions of the people they do employ. Haven't you read about that?"

Cat smiled. "You're talking as if that's something to do with me. It isn't. I don't pay starvation wages."

"So you don't care what happens?"

Cat sighed. "This is only a building, Isabel, for God's sake. What difference does it make if it's a deli or a hair salon?" She paused. "And I have to think of myself. You think of yourself, don't you?"

She stared at Isabel, who lowered her eyes. She was hating this. She hated this sort of conflict.

But Cat was getting into her stride. "You go round lecturing other people but you're all right, aren't you? You've got that house of yours and Grace to look after it for you. And you've got your sexy husband, which is all very nice . . . for you."

Isabel turned away, and did not see the look

that accompanied this last remark. This was ancient business, a combination of unresolved jealousy and resentment; quite impervious, it seemed, to the healing effect of time. It was about something very dark and elemental. It was poison that had not been released by any lance and only now was making its toxic presence felt.

Isabel wondered how to respond, but decided that there was little point; already Eddie was beginning to look in their direction in a worried way. Did he suspect that something was in the offing? Cat would have to tell him, thought Isabel. That was one piece of dirty work she would have to do for herself. And Isabel had just arrived at a more wide-reaching conclusion: she could not take the troubles of the world on her shoulders. She was going to simplify her life by doing what Jamie had long urged her to do. She would get in touch with Iain Melrose and ask him to release her from the obligation she had assumed. If he declined, which she thought rather unlikely, she would do what she had promised to do for him, but she did not see how he could hold her to an undertaking that she now so strongly wished to abandon. And she would disentangle herself, too, from Cat's affairs in general, and from the delicatessen in particular. That would leave Eddie at Cat's mercy, of course, and she was unhappy about that. But what could she do? Where were the boundaries of your moral responsibility for others? Draw those too generously, and life became impossible because you simply could not cope with the demands, emotional and practical, placed upon you. Draw them too narrowly, and your world became a cold and constrained place.

CHAPTER TEN

ISABEL DECIDED to stay a further half an hour before informing Cat that she would not be staying to help during the lunchtime rush. It seemed that Cat half expected this, as she said that she had spoken to Leo, who would be happy to lend a hand. Isabel sensed that Cat was experiencing some regret over their earlier exchange, as her tone was placatory. There was even an apology—or semi-apology—when she said, "I spoke a bit hurriedly this morning. I shouldn't have. But I know you understand."

Isabel made a non-committal reply, and then, shortly after twelve, hung up her apron and prepared to leave the deli.

Eddie was concerned. "Did she say something to you?" he asked. "I saw the two of you having a go at each other."

"There was a disagreement—that's all," she reassured him.

"She can be really crabby at times," Eddie said. "And I think he makes her worse. He's so pleased with himself." He paused. "I think they're planning something."

Isabel busied herself with the removal of her latex gloves.

"Do you know what it is?" Eddie pressed.

Isabel had one glove off; now she tackled the other.

"You should use talcum powder," said Eddie. "They're meant to have it inside the gloves, but they never seem to have enough."

Isabel did not answer his question. She did not have the heart to tell him, and yet she knew she should—particularly if he asked a direct question to which she knew the answer.

"Do you think they're going to sell up?"

Isabel did not meet his gaze at first. But then she turned to him and said, "What do you think?"

"I think they are," he said. "They had some guy in the other day who measured everything with one of those electronic tape measures— you know, the type you point at things and get a reading. He went over the whole place."

Isabel swallowed hard. "I think they might, Eddie. In fact, I think it highly likely."

She watched for his reaction. He was staring at his hands. She waited.

"I'm finished if they do," he said.

"Oh, Eddie, don't say that."

"No, I am, Isabel. I'm finished."

She reached out to touch his forearm. He pulled away.

"You don't know what's going to happen, Eddie. And anyway, you could always get another job. There are all sorts of things you could do."

"I don't think so. You go and speak to people looking for jobs at the moment. They write hundreds of applications—hundreds— and they hardly get any replies."

She waited a few moments before saying anything further. "I'll make sure you get something, Eddie. You aren't alone, you know."

She thought: I've just assumed responsibility

for Eddie. But he said, "You won't be able to. You can't make jobs out of nothing."

"If needs be, I'll help you look for something. I promise you I will."

He moved towards the counter. "I hate him," he said. "It's his fault. She wouldn't be doing this if it weren't for him. I hope he dies."

"Eddie!" whispered Isabel. "You should never say that. Because you don't really, do you?"

"I mean it. I mean it. In fact . . ."

Eddie picked up a knife from beside the cheese board. "See this, Isabel? I could stick this into him. Right in."

Her blood ran cold. This was exactly how it happened. Anger. A knife. A story as old and familiar as Cain's. "Eddie!"

"I swear I could. He laughed when he got me in the eye, didn't he? Well, he won't laugh when I get him back."

Isabel took a step forward. She took the knife from his hand. There was no resistance. "You didn't mean that, did you?"

He said nothing.

"I said: You didn't mean that, did you, Eddie?"

Now he shook his head. "Okay, I was just thinking."

She approached closer and slipped an arm about his shoulder. He did not move away or resist. He felt bony—like a young boy.

"Don't think those thoughts, Eddie. Promise me: don't think them."

His voice was almost inaudible. "I won't."

"Good. Now, I have to go, but I'll drop in and see you on Monday, all right? And if you want to phone me over the weekend, you can do that."

"I won't need to."

"All right. But if you feel at all low, or upset—anything—just call me." She gave him a look that she hoped would impress upon him the fact that she meant what she said. "And I'm sure that Cat is going to talk to you about what's planned. It may not be as bad as you feared."

She went into Cat's office without knocking. Leo was standing near the filing cabinet, supporting Cat, who was hanging on to his neck, her legs wound round his trunk. When Isabel entered, Cat looked over her shoulder and slowly lowered herself. Leo smirked.

"I think you should talk to Eddie," said Isabel. "He's tumbled to what's going on."

Cat frowned. "Did you tell him?"

"I did not," said Isabel. "He's no fool. He's put two and two together."

"I'll talk to him," offered Leo.

"I don't think you should," said Isabel. "I don't think that would be wise."

"I'll talk," said Cat.

"All right," said Isabel, and turned to leave, closing the door behind her. She heard laughter.

SHE HAD TELEPHONED Jamie to tell him she would be coming home early and wanted some private time to talk. He would be back with the boys by then, he said, and he would prepare lunch: macaroni cheese for the boys, and a salad for the two of them. Magnus still had a midday sleep, and when he was off, Charlie could be entertained with a film. There was a strict screen-time policy enforced in the house, but Jamie sensed that this was an occasion for flexibility. "Is everything all right?" he asked anxiously. Isabel assured him it was, but then said, "Or not quite, but I need time to talk to you about . . . well, everything, I suppose. A bombshell from Cat and Leo, to start with, and then, well, my complications."

He knew what she meant by **complications.** He had introduced the word into their private vocabulary himself, to cover the situations that arose when Isabel agreed to sort out people's problems. She did that time and time again, and it seemed to Jamie that although she often brought matters to a satisfactory conclusion for the people she was trying to help, it was often at considerable personal cost—and now and then, even at risk of harm to herself. He lived with this, and indeed in a sense was even proud of it, but if she was planning to extract herself from one of these complications, then he would be more than happy to support her in that.

"Anything you want," he said. "We can talk about everything."

When he saw her, he realised that things were more serious than he had imagined. Isabel looked shaken, and when he took her hands and held her to him, he felt her quiver, as if she was on the verge of tears.

Lunch for the boys was a quick meal, made speedier by unashamed bribery. If the macaroni cheese was finished in ten minutes, Jamie promised them, there would be not one piece of chocolate, but two. And if Magnus went to his rest without any fuss, there would be more chocolate later on, and for his brother too, who would be rewarded if he watched **Mary Poppins** from start to finish without demur. The bargains sealed, Jamie and Isabel soon sat down to their own lunch, the salad that Jamie had prepared earlier on. Isabel toyed with it; she was not in the mood to eat.

She told him about her conversation with Leo and her subsequent discussion with Cat. And then she told him that she had been thinking about Iain Melrose's request and that this, on top of everything else, was just too much for her to handle. "And there's a pile of proofs in the office, waiting for me to look at them. The printer says if he doesn't get them by Tuesday, he can't guarantee that we'll meet the overseas mailing deadline. And if we miss that, then we get into trouble with the library suppliers, who say that we've been late twice in the last two years and . . ." She stopped.

Jamie reached across the table and took her hand. "I know," he said. "I know how much you do."

"And I feel that I'm neglecting the boys," Isabel went on. "I'm their mother and I keep asking Grace to take them or do this or that with them. Or you. You have your rehearsals and concerts and everything, and I know the pressure you can be under. And yet I expect you to be on hand, ready to pick things up when I'm doing something else."

"Most of which," Jamie interrupted, "is things for other people."

"That's not the point."

"I think it's **part** of the point," said Jamie. "And as far as I'm concerned, it's my job anyway. I'm their father. I'm not complaining." He paused. "Anyway, I know how you must feel. All that I want now is for you to do something about it."

Isabel nodded mutely.

"I suggest we go and see Iain Melrose," said Jamie. "You and I together. We go to see him and get you out of that. That at least will clear the decks for us to deal with this whole Cat and Leo business. Agreed?"

Again, Isabel nodded. "I feel bad about it."

"Nonsense," retorted Jamie. "He's the one who should feel bad—imposing on you like that."

"He's a dying man," said Isabel. "And I think he's a good man too. He has the interests of that place up in Argyll at heart."

"Fine," said Jamie. "But he needs to sort it out himself. He needs to make his own decision about these people he can't choose between. We all have to do that sort of thing from time to time. I have to choose who gets the solo slots at the school concerts."

"And I take it that won't be Mark Brogan," said Isabel.

The remark dispelled the tension. Jamie laughed. "Oh, Mark, poor Mark. He's not doing too badly, actually. I think he's been inspired by being put in the school orchestra. It's had a positive effect on his playing."

"Give him a solo slot then," said Isabel.

Jamie laughed. "You're not serious."

But she was. "Think of what it would mean to his mother. She'd burst with pride."

Jamie hesitated, and Isabel pressed him again. "Does it matter?" she asked. "When you

look at these things **sub specie aeternitatis**—
does it matter?"

"It doesn't," Jamie conceded. "Apply that
happiness test of yours . . ."

Isabel objected. "I'm not a utilitarian. Or
not in the crude sense."

"All right, but you have to admit that in this
case it would give great happiness . . . People
like hearing others struggling with an instru-
ment. And the parents would like it too, as
they'd all be thinking: At least ours aren't
that bad."

"So, it's agreed?" said Isabel. "A solo spot
for Mark Brogan at the next school concert?"

"He's on," said Jamie, with a smile.

They went on to discuss the deli. "We keep
out of that," said Jamie. "You want to simplify your life—well, you start by keeping out
of Cat's affairs. If she wants to go off to live
on a boat in Oban or wherever, then that's
her business."

Isabel reluctantly agreed. "But what
about the trust? She's going to make another
application."

Jamie thought for a moment. "I'd suggest

that the trust comes up with the cash. A one-off. Then tell her that's it."

Isabel was doubtful. "But doesn't it strike you as odd that this massive liquidation of assets comes hot on the heels of her engagement to Leo? He's obviously the one behind it. I think he's probably been wanting an expensive yacht for some time and, bingo, here's the way to get it. It's called asset stripping, and Cat's the one who's having all her assets stripped."

Jamie said he understood that was what was occurring. "Things happen," he said. "We don't like all of them."

Isabel reflected that sometimes she liked very little of what was happening in the world.

"But you have to accept things," Jamie insisted. He remembered Isabel saying something about the Stoics and acceptance. "Didn't the Stoics say, 'Accept what you can't influence or change'?"

"They did, and that was my dentist," said Isabel, with a smile. "I told you about our conversation the other day. He'd been reading about the Stoics and mindfulness."

Jamie remembered. "My own dentist says

nothing about philosophy," he reflected. "She only talks about teeth. She uses the word **we** for me. **How are our teeth today? Have we been flossing regularly?**"

"The inclusive first-person plural," said Isabel. "It's well meant, but condescending because . . ." She paused, to think of just why the use of **we** should be wrong. At last, she said, "It's because it removes autonomy of judgement. The person you address in that way is not being given the opportunity to dissent. He—or she—is being **roped in** to a consensus."

"Roped in?"

"Yes. **Have we been flossing regularly?** The sub-text there is: **You have no option— you have to floss regularly—and you know it because you and I are part of a greater we.**"

Jamie burst out laughing. "You can make simple things beautifully complicated—you really can."

"Thank you," said Isabel. "And you can uncomplicate them."

"That's exactly what I'm trying to do," said Jamie.

"And succeeding," said Isabel.

She rose from her place at the table, put her arms around Jamie and kissed him. "Thank you," she said.

She felt as if a burden had been lifted, which it had. Life was suddenly simpler, less onerous. All that was required now was a couple of conversations, a few days with the guilt pile in her study, and an uninterrupted night of sleep. There was something else, and it bothered her that she could not remember it. But then she did. The dental hygienist. Her dentist had told her to make an appointment with the dental hygienist and she had not done so.

"Why are you smiling, Isabel?" asked Jamie. She told him. "I'm smiling because I'm thinking about something unimportant—or no, it's important, because oral hygiene is important—but which is, nonetheless, something I shouldn't be worrying about too much when I'm trying to declutter my life. If you see what I mean."

Jamie kissed her. We assume, thought Isabel, that those whom we kiss have gone regularly to the dental hygienist. And then she thought: Do dental hygienists enjoy kissing, knowing what they know?

"You're smiling again," said Jamie.

IAIN MELROSE had agreed to see them at four o'clock that afternoon. "I used to play golf every Saturday afternoon," he said, "but now it's a bit much for me. So you'll find me in."

His house was in the Braids, a broad hillside on the south side of the city, just before the Pentland Hills sweep down to the Borders. It was on a road of large Victorian houses, each surrounded by a substantial garden—houses that had been constructed in Edwardian times for Edinburgh merchants who fancied themselves as country gentlemen but who still needed to be within reach of town. The houses bore evocative names, sometimes etched in stone on the gateposts: here was Inverness House, redolent of the Highlands; here was Russell Lodge, and High Corrie and, poignantly, Ypres.

Iain lived in Stonehaven, a rambling example

of revived Scots baronial architecture. It had been well looked after, the stonework renewed here and there with the insertion of a new mullion or lintel, the sills of the windows painted fresh white, the gravel at the side of the house recently and neatly raked. He had been looking out for their arrival, and as Isabel drove her green Swedish car up the short driveway to the house, Iain was there to greet them at the front door.

He led them into the drawing room. "I should have entertained you before this," he said. "I've become . . . well, not as social as I used to be."

Isabel looked about the room. It was comfortable, rather than affluent, although there was the solidity that goes with understated wealth: the family photographs on the side table were in silver frames; the fireplace was carved Edinburgh pine of a type much appreciated by specialists in such things, with seashells, anchors and a harvest scene delicately moulded and applied to the wood. There were several paintings on the walls that she was sure were Fergussons, while one, a view of Ben More on Mull, was a Peploe. The thought

came to her mind of how hard it must be to leave the small things one loves: the painting one's become attached to and looks at every day; the favourite teacup that you've drunk out of at the breakfast table for years and years; our small links with the world. And how pressing, then, must become the urge to do something to perpetuate that relationship with that which is loved; to have an heir; to know what is going to happen to your possessions. Or did you accept that all these things were part of a world that you were leaving; that they were not yours in any permanent sense, because there was no such thing as permanence?

A photograph on a smaller side table caught her eye. There were two people in it—Iain and his wife, she assumed. Iain was wearing a kilt and the woman was in jeans and a green waxed Barbour jacket. Their hair was ruffled by the wind. There was a mountain behind them. That was Argyll, she thought, and that was his happiness.

He saw her looking. "Yes," he said. "That was taken about six years ago. You'll see the hill behind us."

Isabel, permitted now to stare, took a closer look at the photograph.

"The section off to the left is forested now," he said. "We did a big planting a few years ago. We've put in broadleaf trees. There were some generous grants available."

He offered the tea, which was already in the room, on a tray near the window. Then they sat down and Isabel exchanged a glance with Jamie.

"I'm sorry to eat into your Saturday afternoon," Isabel began, "but I wanted to . . ." She hesitated, but then continued, "I wanted to ask you to release me from what I agreed to do."

Iain did not seem surprised. He inclined his head slightly, and then put down his teacup. "I can't say this comes as a shock," he said. "In fact, would you believe me if I said I was going to make the same request of you?"

It took Isabel a few moments to take this in. "You mean, you don't want me to do it?"

"Yes, I do mean that," said Iain. "I feel that I should never have asked you in the first place. It was grossly presumptuous."

Jamie cleared his throat. "Actually," he said, "you'd be surprised how often Isabel gets asked to do this sort of thing."

Iain smiled. "Her reputation precedes her."

"Jamie says I agree too readily," said Isabel. "And perhaps I do. Then I become overwhelmed and it all gets a bit much."

"Well," Iain said, "this is one occasion when that won't happen. And I really am sorry for burdening you."

Isabel wondered whether he had made alternative arrangements. "Have you managed to sort it out?" she asked.

Iain shook his head. "No. I shall be having a word with the lawyers on Monday. They'll come up with something."

There was a brief silence. Then Iain said, "I hope you enjoyed meeting Jack the other night. I liked the exhibition."

"We both did," said Isabel. "Jamie likes his work—as do I."

"He's very talented," said Iain.

"I'm sorry I didn't meet your other cousins," said Isabel.

"Sarah and John?"

"Yes. She's the property person, isn't she? You did say that was what she did, didn't you?"

"Yes," said Iain. "She's actually a builder by trade. It's unusual—even today—to find a woman builder, but that was her background. Then she started to do flats up and keep them for rental purposes. She has quite a number of them now—ten or twelve, I believe. But she still does renovations.

"And you didn't meet John either," Iain went on. "He's the accountant. He's the one I know the least well, I suppose, although we occasionally play golf together. He has a passion for history. He loves the Portrait Gallery. He knows the background story of just about everyone depicted in the portraits there. He's a quiet man. Not particularly happy, I think."

Isabel waited. She had come here to extricate herself, not to engage, but already she felt the draw.

"I shouldn't be speculating," said Iain, "but when you're in my position, as it were, you feel you can speak more freely."

"Of course," said Isabel.

"John's probably not interested in women,

but doesn't care to advertise it. That's his prerogative, in my view. Do we need to know about everybody's private affairs? Not in my view."

"Nor mine," said Jamie.

"I think he's one of those people who could have been either," went on Iain. "It just so happened that at an important time in his life he fell for one person rather than another. He had a friend when he was a teenager and I think he never really got over him. It was a David and Jonathan friendship, and Jonathan went off and got married and moved to Glasgow and David, well, he never felt that way about anybody else. Ever. It's very sad."

"Yes," said Isabel. "And there are lots of lives like that, I think. Lives of all sorts— people who've loved somebody and it hasn't been reciprocated and yet they've carried on loving them from a distance all their lives."

"A real shame," said Jamie. "It's a pity we can't do something to equalise things, in a way." He paused. "Isabel and I sometimes talk about utilitarianism, you know. That's about happiness and spreading it to the maximum number of people."

Iain smiled and turned to Isabel. "I suppose that's what it's like to be married to a philosopher."

Jamie took a sip of his tea. "But we did meet Jack and Hilary, didn't we?"

Iain frowned. "You did, yes. At the gallery."

Jamie looked quickly at Isabel, who seemed uncertain as to what to expect. She gave him a quizzical look, which he did not return.

"Isabel had met Hilary before," he said.

Iain was listening. "Oh yes?"

"On jury service," said Jamie.

Isabel interrupted him. "Jamie, I don't think we should talk about that."

But Iain's interest was aroused. "About what? About being on a jury together?"

"That's meant to be confidential," said Isabel. "What happens in the jury room shouldn't be discussed outside."

"Yes, but this is important," said Jamie.

Isabel tried again: "Jamie . . ."

"She saw Hilary with the man who was on trial," Jamie continued. "Later—after he had been acquitted."

Iain sat quite still. "I'm dismayed to hear this," he said.

"There could have been an innocent explanation," Isabel protested.

"Unlikely," Jamie said quietly.

"Jack's all right," Iain said, as if to himself.
"But he's putty in her hands."

"What about Sarah?" Jamie suddenly
asked. "Do you like her?"

"It's not a question of whom I like," said
Iain. "That's not the point here. It's a question
of who's **best.**"

"Is she greedy?" asked Jamie.

Iain was taken aback by the question. "You
mean—at the table?"

"No, not that. Is she selfish? Sometimes
these property developers are a bit, how shall
one put it . . . Well, **greedy** might be the word."

Iain laughed. "She probably is. In fact, yes,
she is. She seems determined to build up her
property portfolio."

"She's a businesswoman," Isabel pointed
out. "That's what they do." She fixed Jamie
with an intense stare. "And anyway, none of
this is any of our business now."

But Jamie seemed to have the bit between
his teeth. "Have you spoken to her tenants?"
he asked.

"Jamie," said Isabel. "This is nothing to do with us."

Iain shook his head. "No. I haven't."

"Because that might tell you everything you need to know," said Jamie. "And if they say that she's a good landlord, responsive to their needs and so on, then that gives you one answer. But if they say that she seems determined to get as much rent out of them as possible with minimum input on her part, you have your answer there."

"Perhaps," said Iain.

Isabel was looking at Jamie with frank astonishment. Turning to Iain, she said, "We didn't come here to tell you what to do."

"But since we're here," interjected Jamie, "we may as well give you our views. And would you like to know who I think should get this? Would you?"

Iain smiled. "It looks as if you're going to tell me."

"John," said Jamie.

THEY GOT INTO the car in silence. Then, as she pulled out of the drive, Isabel half turned to Jamie. "What possessed you?" she asked.

Jamie kept looking fixedly out of the passenger window. "I don't know," he said. "I really don't. It just all welled up. I suddenly felt sorry for him, I suppose. There he is—he's dying—and he wanted our help."

"Which you told me—"

He cut her short. "I know, I know. I said you shouldn't get involved. But then, when we were actually there, sitting with him, with his things around us . . . that photograph of him and his wife . . . that funny stuffed leather pig for putting your feet on . . . all of that, I thought, here he is faced with a decision that he couldn't seem to get his head round, and we knew something that was relevant, and . . ."

Isabel drew into the side of the road. She stopped the engine. They were under a tree, and the shadow of its branches moved across the windscreen. It was warm, and they could see the tops of the Pentlands in a light haze of heat.

"I know what you mean," Isabel said quietly.

Jamie bit his lip. "You can't be in this world

without feeling something," he said. "You have to feel it."

Her tone was resigned—a tone of sadness. "I'm afraid that's true. And once you start to feel the pain of the world, then, oh God, it's hard to stop feeling it."

Jamie turned to face her. "And people—people like me—don't make it any easier if they come along and tell you not to get involved."

"But you have to," said Isabel. "Because I get myself into these terrible spins if you don't."

He knew that was true—it was what he had argued for a long time. But he had just acted contrary to that position—and he was glad that he had.

"I don't know what we've done back there," he said. "I think we've sown some seeds."

Isabel was more certain. "We've decided it," she said. "Hilary is a spent force—and she wrecks it for Jack, whatever his claims might be. Sarah is put under suspicion of being a grubby developer—the last person you'd want to give a sensitive estate to. And that leaves John, whom we've never met, but whom you seem to have identified as the one to choose."

"I had a feeling he was," said Jamie.

"Somebody who loves another person all his life when he knows it's impossible. Someone who likes the Scottish National Portrait Gallery. Somebody who doesn't say very much. What's wrong with him?"

"Nothing, as far as I can see," said Isabel. "But we're hardly basing our views on any substantial evidence."

"Don't you think," asked Jamie, "that he already knew? That at some level Iain knows what the right decision is, but just needed somebody to help him see that."

Isabel thought that quite likely. She looked at her watch. "Grace," she said. "We'd better go and relieve her."

"She doesn't mind how late we are," said Jamie. "We could go for a walk on Braid Hill. Just you and me, and the wind."

"We could."

"And we could think about how lucky we are. Because neither of us is signing off from this world—just yet—and we have the boys and music and philosophy."

"And Brother Fox."

"Yes," agreed Jamie. "And Brother Fox."

"And he has us."

Jamie shook his head. "I don't think he knows that. I suppose you can have people—and things—but not know that you have them."

Isabel switched on the engine. "Like guardian angels? Some people are convinced they have a guardian angel watching over them."

"I'm not," said Jamie. "And I imagine you aren't either."

"True," said Isabel. "It's a nice idea, of course, but . . ."

They began to move off slowly. Something made Isabel turn her head, though, and she saw that a car was coming up fast behind them. She depressed the brake quickly and firmly, and avoided a collision. She looked at Jamie.

He had not felt the unseen hand that had touched her.

"Orlando Gibbons," mused Jamie.

Isabel was distracted. She was thinking about what had just happened, but said, "What about him?"

"He wrote a lovely anthem for when James VI came back to Scotland for the first time after taking the English throne. There are a couple of lines in it that I rather like. The choir at school sang it the other day— really rather well. **Oh, send thine angels to his blessed side / And bid them there abide.** It sounds like a request for reinforcements."

Isabel liked the metaphor. We all needed reinforcements, she thought. We wanted others to think the way we did, to protest the values we held dear, to keep at bay the things we thought needed to be kept at bay. If imaginary beings could help to keep our courage up, then there was no harm in that.

"I think we should go for that walk," she said. "Tell me where to go."

"Straight ahead," said Jamie. "Then turn right when you get to the place where you have to turn right."

She smiled, and slipped a hand across to put on his knee. She squeezed it gently.

"Driving under the influence of love," she muttered.

They parked the car at the foot of Braid Hill and were soon up on the high moor, overlooking the city. Edinburgh stretched before them—rooftops, church spires, the crouching lion of Arthur's Seat, the craggy spine of the Castle and the descending High Street. The wind was from the east, fresh from the iron-blue fields of the North Sea, the tiniest hint of salt in its eyes.

Isabel held Jamie's hand as they walked. "I've been thinking of something," she said. "Will you let me at least raise it with you without your jumping down my throat?"

He put an arm about her. "When did I ever do that?" he asked.

"Never," she said. "But there's always a first time."

"Tell me what it is."

She told him, and he understood.

CHAPTER ELEVEN

❖

I SUPPOSE," said Hamish MacGeorge, "that we should be formal. Or at least, we should formally constitute the meeting." He busied himself with a sheet of paper. "I shall be secretary, if Gordon is all right with that."

"I'm happy for you to be Grand Panjandrum," said Gordon MacGregor. "If that's what you want."

"Secretary will suffice," said Hamish. And then, turning to Isabel, he said, "I shall record Jamie's presence with us, although technically, since he isn't a trustee, he shouldn't perhaps speak—if you don't mind my saying so."

"He can speak, but not participate in decisions," said Gordon. "There's a distinction there. He can give the trustees his views, but may not actually vote on anything. That's not to say that his views will not be taken fully into account."

Bemused by the pedantry of the two lawyers, Jamie grinned broadly. "I'm fine with just sitting here," he said. "I don't mind."

"Of course, many people who wield power have advisers in the background," said Gordon. "Mary, Queen of Scots, was apparently very attentive to what Rizzio had to say."

"Not that that did him much good," said Hamish. "And there are times when it's a good thing that people **don't** listen. I like reading political history, and I've just been reading about President John F. Kennedy."

"A terribly nice man," said Gordon, shaking his head. "That was a tragic business in Dallas."

"Oh, it certainly was," agreed Hamish. "But the interesting thing is this: President Kennedy stood up to people, apparently. He wouldn't be pushed around. And so when General Curtis LeMay tried to persuade him to attack Russian sites in Cuba, he resisted. LeMay wanted a war with the Soviet

Union. Fortunately, Kennedy refused to be browbeaten."

"We were almost reduced to dust," said Gordon. "The whole world was almost incinerated."

"And that was not the only time," Hamish said. "There was the time that Russian colonel overrode the radar warning systems. If he had acted according to the book, he would have pressed the button for a response to what was coming up as a missile attack from the United States, and we wouldn't be here today."

"Two men who saved the world," said Isabel. "But I suppose we should get on with the business in hand." She thought: The trust was paying for every minute of Hamish and Gordon's time. Every excursus on Scottish country dancing or nuclear politics was re-corded on the time sheets, not as idle chatter or reminiscence, but as professional consultation.

Hamish said, "We have the Land Rover matter on the agenda. We've acted on that as instructed."

"Yes," said Isabel. "But there's more."

She told them about her conversations with Cat and Leo and the plan to market the deli.

At the end of that, Hamish shook his head vigorously. "The Land Rover request is out of order now, I think." He looked at Gordon for support. Gordon nodded. "If she's selling the business, then she does not need a Land Rover. We should retract our agreement." He turned to Isabel. "Would you not agree with that, Isabel?"

She did not reply immediately. A case could be made out, she thought, for regarding the vehicle as pertaining to the next business— the boat charter concern. Support for that would be within the scope of the original trust purposes, she imagined. The founding deed had referred to "any business" in which Cat was engaged, and the boat would clearly fall within that definition.

It was Jamie, though, who made that point for her. And when he finished, Hamish and Gordon both seemed to see the force of it.

"But she's intending to ask for something else," said Isabel. "You won't have received it yet, but I think you should stand by for a request for one hundred thousand, or there-abouts, to assist in the purchase of the boat I told you about."

"One hundred thousand pounds is a lot of money," said Gordon. "Put that together with fifty thousand for the Land Rover and it makes a major sum."

"Can the trust afford it?" asked Isabel.

Hamish and Gordon exchanged amused glances. "Not being able to afford something is not a problem this trust has," said Hamish.

Jamie now spoke for the first time. "So, you wouldn't notice it?"

Hamish turned to him. "Oh, we'd notice it," he said. "Our philosophy in this firm is to notice **everything.** Every penny that moves through our accounts is . . . is observed and entered in the appropriate column. But whether we would **feel** it is a different matter."

"And the answer to that is no," interjected Gordon.

"May I ask you something?" said Hamish.

Isabel nodded. "Yes, of course."

"Do you believe this young man, this Leo, is trying to get hold of your niece's money? When it comes down to it, is that why he's asked her to marry him?"

"Yes," said Jamie. "But—"

"No," said Isabel.

Gordon smiled. "I see we have a difference of opinion."

"Well, he is and he isn't," said Isabel. "I think the two of them are probably in love. They clearly enjoy one another's company." She thought of how she had walked in on Cat when she was draped around Leo. "They **are** lovers, after all."

Gordon blushed. "I don't think any of us were in any doubt about that side of things."

"I think that they established their relationship before he knew about Cat's situation," said Isabel. "Then, when it became obvious that there were funds in the background, he decided to take advantage."

Jamie said he would, broadly speaking, go along with that hypothesis.

"So, it's not clear-cut," said Hamish.

Isabel said that indeed, she thought it was not. "Jamie and I are coming round to the view that we should accede to these two requests—the vehicle and the boat—and then make it clear that that is the limit of the trust's support. In that way I won't be heading for a complete rupture of relations with Cat—something I would strongly wish to avoid—because there's something I want Cat's co-operation over."

"Of course," said Hamish. "Nobody wants disagreement. And I imagine that Gordon and I will be very happy to go along with you in that decision."

Now Isabel brought up the other matter she had wanted discussed. "I mentioned to you that they were thinking of selling the deli to a hairdresser."

Gordon looked at a note he had made on a piece of paper. "A Mr. Jonny Mustique," he said. "Yes, you mentioned that. An unusual name, I must say."

"This Jonny Mustique is prepared to offer for the premises," Isabel said. "But I was wondering—well, Jamie and I were both wondering—whether the trust could buy the deli lock, stock and barrel. We've had a preliminary discussion ourselves, and we wanted to sound you out."

Hamish made a small round hole of his lips and exhaled quickly. "Buy the deli?"

"Yes," said Isabel. "I gather that the existing trust portfolio includes a couple of shops

somewhere—and a warehouse. They're assets, are they not?"

"Well, they are, yes," said Hamish. "They're what we call immoveable property. And trusts are perfectly competent owners of immoveable property."

Isabel looked from lawyer to lawyer. "So you see no legal reason why we can't acquire Cat's deli—at its market price, of course?"

Hamish saw no reason to preclude this, and neither did Gordon.

"Of course," said Hamish, "it would not be open to us as trustees to make a bad investment if it were perfectly obvious that it was not a good prospect. But I take it that Cat's deli is thriving?"

"It is," said Jamie. "It makes a reasonable profit, doesn't it, Isabel?"

Hamish shrugged. "Then, in theory, we could make a bid for it. But who would run it? I know you work there from time to time, Isabel, but would you have the time to run it yourself?"

For a few moments nobody said anything. Isabel and Jamie had discussed this earlier,

when Isabel had first floated the idea on their walk. "I could get it up and running," she had said. "I know my way around. And then we could appoint a manager to work with Eddie."

Jamie had sighed. "If I thought there was any point in trying to persuade you not to do this, I would," he said. "But this is just too important for you, isn't it?"

She told him it was. "It's mostly about Eddie," she said.

"I understand. And in this particular case, I'm with you."

"He's got nobody, you see—except us."

Jamie made a gesture of acceptance. "Temporarily, then?"

"Yes," she said. "Temporarily."

Now Isabel answered Hamish's question. "I shall run it in the first instance," she said. "With help, of course. We already have a perfectly capable young man working there. I suspect he'd appreciate more responsibility."

Jamie groaned inwardly. Isabel would now have the **Review,** two children, a house, a husband and a delicatessen to manage. He rolled his eyes heavenwards and thought: Stoicism.

Did it help? He was not sure, but when Gordon brought in a bottle of sherry and the soda-water syphon at the end of the meeting, Jamie accepted a glass with a degree of relief.

"To the success of this new venture," Hamish said, raising his glass.

"We must purchase it first," said Gordon. "And in my experience, it doesn't do to celebrate prematurely."

Hamish nodded sagely. "Good advice," he said. "Until you have the property deed in your hand, the contract signed, the banker's draft paid into the account, the court order pronounced and so on—until you have these things actually in your grasp, anything can go wrong." He raised his small glass of sherry and soda water to his lips. "And it often does, doesn't it, Gordon?"

"Oh my," said Gordon. "It certainly does, Hamish."

"It sounds as if your firm should perhaps be called Messrs. Jeremiah and Jeremiah, WS," said Isabel.

The two lawyers both burst out laughing— a slightly shrill, high-pitched laugh in both cases—a laugh redolent of deed boxes and red document tape and the dust of ancient agreements.

"How very funny," said Hamish.

"I must tell the senior partner," added Gordon. "He loves a joke."

ISABEL MANAGED to snatch a couple of hours later that afternoon to concentrate on the **Review.** She worked quickly and with a degree of concentration that she would have found difficult to muster had her mind not been put at rest by Hamish and Gordon. They had been completely accommodating at the trustees' meeting, and when she and Jamie had left the lawyers' office, they both felt that the Cat issue had been more or less defused. That, coupled with the easy exit Isabel had found from her entanglement with Iain Melrose, made her feel that her life was now both simpler and considerably less stressful.

She was coming to the end of her working session, shortly after five, when she saw the courier walking up the path that led to the front door. Leaving her desk, she was at the door when he pressed the bell. He was her regular from Eagle Couriers, a young man called Steve, with whom she often exchanged the time of day when he made a delivery or picked up a parcel.

"What do you have for me this evening, Steve?" she asked. "More books, I assume."

Steve produced a small rectangular parcel. "Nope," he said. "This is marked fragile."

He handed her the parcel. Through the protective wrapping she could tell that it was a framed object of some sort.

"A nice change," she said, as she signed Steve's machine, her fingernail tracing an indecipherable squiggle across the screen.

He left her and she went inside with her parcel. There was no note on the outside, just her name written on the wrapping in an elegant italic script. She removed this layer and the plastic bubble-wrap underneath it.

It was, as she had suspected, a painting, framed in an expensive-looking gilt frame. On the back was a gallery label: The Scottish Gallery: Jack Reay, **Machair, South Uist.**

She turned the picture over. A delicate picture, worked in oil pastels, and protected by glass. It showed a stretch of foreshore: sand, shells, wildflowers, a green sea, white crest tumbling. This was **machair,** that quintessentially Hebridean landscape—part beach, part sand dune, part field of tiny flowers.

She stared at it. She could smell the land it represented. She could hear the cold sea falling upon its broken shells and sand.

There was an envelope taped to the back of the painting, again with her name in italic script. She opened this.

Dear Isabel,

Time always conspires against us, no matter how organised we try to be—do you find that? I had intended to invite you and Jamie (do I have the name right?) for kitchen supper over here at the house, and then, looking at the diary, I saw a whole lot of inflexible engagements. Hopeless. However, I am determined we should do that, and I'll be getting in touch to find a convenient evening for the two of you.

In the meantime, though, I thought you might appreciate this little painting.

Jack did it a couple of years ago when we went over to Barra and the Uists. It was summer—a gorgeous spell in which the rain, by some miracle, held off for a full two weeks. He managed to do a lot of painting, and this little oil pastel is one of the things he did. I could tell, at the opening the other evening, that you liked his work and so I thought you might appreciate this little gift. Both Jack and I like the thought of it being in your house rather than being whisked off to Dubai or somewhere like that.

No need to acknowledge. I hope that you find a place for it somewhere on your walls. Until very soon, I hope,

Hilary Reay

Isabel put the painting down on the hall table. She glanced at it again, and then made her way through to the kitchen, where she had heard Jamie making the boys' supper, while they played on the floor with a wooden toy railway. There was some sort of dispute going on as to the ownership of a piece of track, and small voices were raised.

"Don't fight," shouted Jamie above the din. "There's enough for everybody."

Isabel thought: Yes, that was true and might be said to all humanity. **Don't fight— there's enough for everybody.** The problem, though, was that not everybody understood the necessary limitations.

Isabel stepped over the chaos at floor level. "A picture has arrived," she said. "A Jack Reay."

Jamie, half concentrating on his cooking, and half on what was happening down below, said, "Jack who?"

"Jack Reay. The opening at the Scottish Gallery."

He stirred a pot of home-made pasta sauce. "Oh yes, of course."

"Sent by his wife, Hilary," said Isabel. "The juror, no less. As a gift, she said."

Jamie looked thoughtful. Then he said, "A bribe, obviously."

"What else can it be?" asked Isabel.

"We must return it. Send it back."

Isabel nodded. "It's lovely, by the way. It's of a stretch of **machair** on South Uist. I could fall in love with it."

"That makes no difference," said Jamie. "It has to go."

"You're right," said Isabel. "But what do I say?"

Jamie shrugged. "You say that you can't accept it. Just that. You don't have to give a reason." He paused, and dipped a spoon into the sauce. "Taste this."

Isabel did. "Lovely."

"We could have it too, if we decided to have pasta tonight. I have some salmon steaks, but there's something about this sauce that makes me want to change my mind and eat what the kids eat."

"Nothing wrong with that," said Isabel.

She turned to go back to the hall to retrieve the painting. As she did so, an idea came to her. It was an outrageous, improbable idea, but it came to her with complete clarity. She returned to Jamie's side.

"Do you remember my mentioning a woman who was a victim of that Macglashian character? The fraudster?"

"Vaguely," said Jamie. "A hairdresser, you said."

"Yes. She was a hairdresser with a son who had cystic fibrosis. I remember her well when she gave evidence in court. She was so brave."

"What about her?" asked Jamie.

"I remember a few details," Isabel said. "She worked in that salon on Morningside Road. You know the big one on the left as you go down towards the clock."

"I can't place it," said Jamie.

"You'll have walked past it," said Isabel. "Anyway, she trained there and was working there six years ago. She might still be there. I remember that her name was Jean—I can't remember her surname."

"Why are you thinking about her now?"

Isabel told him. "She lost everything—all her savings. Well, I have an idea about getting something back for her. Say half of what she lost."

Jamie put down his spoon and replaced the lid on the pot. "How?" he asked.

"We sell this picture we've just been given. You saw the prices at the exhibition. Jack Reay is seriously expensive now."

Jamie smiled. "Rather nice . . . We sell the picture and give her the proceeds."

"Precisely," said Isabel, warming further to the plan by the moment. "I'll speak to Guy about it. It's the sort of thing he'd approve of."

"I assume we have title?" said Jamie. "I don't want to sound like Hamish or Gordon, but we're talking about something quite valuable here."

"I have a letter in her own handwriting," said Isabel. "It's signed by her. She's given it to me. It's what art dealers call a good provenance. In fact, it's a perfect provenance. Watertight."

Jamie's expression was one of deep satisfaction. "Lovely," he said. "And I take it we can tell her what we've done with her gift?"

"I think we should," said Isabel. "Transparency is a great virtue." She looked at her watch. "I can't wait, Jamie. Would you mind if I went to see if that place is still open—the hair salon? I think they don't close till after six."

He understood her impatience. When a good idea occurred to him, he found similar difficulty in waiting. "Go straightaway," he said. "Then go and see Guy, if he's around."

She looked at him in gratitude. "You'll do the supper? And bedtime?"

"The works," he said. "Come back whenever you like."

SHE TOOK the green Swedish car to save time. Parking it near the Dominion Cinema, she made her way down Morningside Road to the Morningside Salon: Hair Stylists Since 1972. She paused outside: inside she could see several customers still being attended to. A young woman sitting at a desk near the window was paging through an appointment register.

She went in and introduced herself to the young woman at the desk. "I'm not here for an appointment," she said. "I wondered if Jean still worked here."

The young woman smiled. "Jean Martin? Yes, she's here. Round the back."

Isabel caught her breath. She had not expected it to be that easy.

"The same Jean Martin?" Isabel asked. "She trained here years ago."

"That's her," said the young woman. "You'll still catch her. She's in the staff room, but she'll be going home in a few minutes, I think. Do you want me to call her?"

Isabel nodded. "Please."

The young woman got up and walked through the salon to a door at the far end. A few minutes later, she reappeared, accompanied by a woman in her mid-forties, wearing blue jeans and a white linen top.

Isabel smiled at her. "You don't know me," she said. "My name is Isabel Dalhousie and I live over there in Merchiston."

Jean's expression was open. She has a friendly face, thought Isabel.

"Oh yes." Her tone was polite—enquiring.

"Some years ago," said Isabel, "I was on the jury in a case at the High Court. You gave evidence. There was a man called Macglashian."

Jean's expression darkened. "Him," she spat out. "He got away with it."

"Not everyone on the jury agreed with that," Isabel whispered. "We're not meant to talk about it, but I can tell you that's how it was."

Jean looked at Isabel mutely. Then she said, "Why are you telling me this?"

"Because I may be in a position—may be—to recover some of the money you lost."

Jean gasped. "Recover . . ."

"Not all, by any means," said Isabel. "And I don't know exactly how much. But I want to try."

Jean was silent. Isabel noticed that her hands were trembling.

"I've rather sprung this on you," said Isabel.

"Aye," said Jean. "I haven't thought about it for some time. I thought it best to forget it. And it's making me feel a bit . . ."

"Of course it is," said Isabel. "But look, I'm going to give you my phone number and my email address. Can you give me yours?"

"Of course."

They took the pieces of paper that the young woman at the desk, who had listened discreetly to their conversation, tore out of a notebook and gave them. Each wrote out their details and passed them to the other.

"I can't believe this is happening," said Jean. "I really can't."

Isabel smiled. "I find it a bit difficult to believe too," she said.

After she had walked back up from the salon, she drove across town to Dundas Street. She had called Guy Peploe on her mobile and he had invited her to meet him at his flat round the corner. Guy's son let her in. "You're the philosopher, aren't you?" he said.

"I am," she said. "Your father tells me that philosophy is one of your favourite subjects."

"My absolute favourite," he said. "Have you read Dennett?"

Isabel said she had. "Not recently, though."

"And Roger Scruton?"

"Again, not for some time."

Guy appeared in the hall. "Enough philosophy. Isabel and I need to talk."

"It's refreshing," said Isabel.

"It's been his thing for some three years now," said Guy. "He loves it."

"Perhaps he'll review some books for us," said Isabel.

Guy smiled. "Ask him," he said. "But not this evening. You said you wanted to show me something."

They went into the drawing room, where Isabel extracted the picture and showed it to Guy.

"I've seen this before," said Guy. "He didn't put it in the exhibition, but I know he had it;

I tried to get him to put it on the market, but he's been holding on to it for some reason. It's a real beauty."

He gave Isabel an enquiring look. "Where did you get this? From his studio?"

"It's a very unusual story," replied Isabel. "Do you mind if I tell you the whole thing—from start to finish?"

"I'm listening," said Guy.

When Isabel had finished, Guy looked at her with a mixture of admiration and bemusement. "What an extraordinary set of events," he said. "But then, I've always known that your life was somewhat unconventional."

"My question is this," said Isabel. "Could you sell this for me—and if so, what could I expect? As I said, the money would go to this woman, Jean."

"I understand," said Guy. "And it seems a very fine idea, if I may say so. This painting is definitely your property. That woman is right out of line on this. I've always thought she had Jack under her thumb—she's a sort of Lady Macbeth, in my view. Just between ourselves. On balance, I think he's crossed over to her side, I'm afraid."

"So?" pressed Isabel. "Would it sell?"

"Of course it would," said Guy. "You may not know, but every single picture in the current show sold. I have a list of eight or nine collectors who are pretty keen to get their hands on anything of his. He's been on the up for years now."

"Would one of them take it?" asked Isabel.

"Like a shot," said Guy.

"And how much would we get?"

Guy hesitated. "It's difficult. But I can tell you one thing—we won't take our normal commission on this. This is clearly pro bono. I'll pass on every penny." He paused. "I'd say about twenty-two thousand."

"Jean lost thirty," said Isabel. She was about to add that twenty-two would be more than enough to redress the wrong, but Guy had something to add.

"In that case, I'll ask for twenty-five," he said. "And I wouldn't be surprised if we got it."

"When?" asked Isabel.

Guy looked at his watch. "By ten-thirty?"

Isabel laughed.

"All right," said Guy. "That's perhaps a bit ambitious. But what about next week? I know one of these collectors well. He lives up in Perthshire. I can get him on the phone tomorrow. He doesn't hang around—I suspect we can tie it up. Leave the painting with me and I'll send him an image."

Isabel rose to her feet. "This is marvellous," she said.

"I agree," said Guy. "But then I've heard that this is the sort of thing you do."

Isabel was modest. "Not really," she said. "I usually make a mess of things, but every so often the unexpected occurs and things work out well."

She made her way downstairs and into the summer evening. In a few weeks' time the solstice would be with them, that perfect moment between what had been and what was to come. It would barely get dark then at these northern latitudes, even at midnight; now the sun was still painting the roofs golden at eight o'clock, a gentle presence, a visitor to a Scotland that was more accustomed to short days and wind and drifting, omnipresent rain. And yet was so beautiful, thought Isabel; so beautiful as to break the heart.

CHAPTER TWELVE

❖

CAT HAD MOVED within the last few months to a new flat on Warrender Park Terrace, overlooking the Meadows, the rolling park that divided the old city from its Victorian residential hinterland. The Meadows had been all things to all: a plague burial ground, a loch that provided the city with its drinking water, a golf links, a football ground, a patch of ground for the wartime cultivation of vegetables. Now, lined and intersected by elms and flowering trees, it was a place of summer picnics, festival circuses, snatched moments of courtship, cricket and ecstatic urban dogs released from their leads. Cat's terrace, a towering six-storey Victorian building, topped by crenellations and spikes, was popular with students, who could see the university on the other side of the park, and with young families who liked the generosity of the flats' proportions. Cat had moved to it for the light and for the storage space afforded by its four large bedrooms.

Isabel had heard all about the flat, of course, but the promised invitation to dinner had never materialised. She had not taken that personally—nor had it been intended in that way: Cat's private life had always been slightly chaotic, Isabel thought. There were always crises with deliveries or with the coming and going of tradesmen. The plumber seemed to be in and out, and Cat needed to be there to let him in: Would Isabel mind giving Eddie a hand while she went off to attend to the plumber? And then the painter would be coming to look at the redecoration of the kitchen, and he could only give a rough indication of when he might arrive: Would Isabel mind? And then there were people, friends of Cat's from university days, who were coming to stay, or who suddenly were not because their plans had changed and they would be going to Glasgow instead. And now, of course, there was Leo, who possibly lived with Cat, or possibly did not. Cat had mentioned a flat that she said Leo had down in Leith, but then, a few days later, it was in Newington. If an invitation to dinner did come, Isabel thought, it could quite easily be cancelled because something else had turned up and Cat had to be somewhere else altogether. So Isabel reconciled herself to never seeing the flat in Warrender Park Terrace, even if she had a fairly good theoretical idea of what it was like.

But that morning, having telephoned Eddie and been told that Cat was not in the deli as she was expecting a new washing machine to be installed, Isabel made a decision. Cat had said that she would be in at lunchtime, Eddie said, and that if he needed her he could call her at the flat. Isabel knew that if she arranged a meeting with Cat it would be unlikely to be that day. She did not want to see her in the deli, as she was unwilling to have the discussion she was planning to have with Cat within earshot of Eddie. This discussion, after all, was all about Eddie and his future, and she did not want to raise his hopes before anything firmer had been arranged.

So she decided to visit Cat, unannounced, in her flat on Warrender Park Terrace. She had the address, and it was barely fifteen minutes' walk away from La Barantine, where she had her morning coffee and bought the day's baguette and French country loaf.

Now she stood in front of a dark red door on the fourth floor of Cat's tenement building. The original door furniture had been well preserved: a heavy Victorian door handle, a brass knocker in the shape of a thistle, and, although a recent addition, no doubt a replacement for a dynasty of similar pieces—a gleaming brass plate with the name DALHOUSIE in capitals in its centre. To the right of the door, inlaid in the jamb, was a small, modern bell-button. Isabel pushed this, and heard a chime somewhere within the flat. Then silence. After a minute or so, she pressed the button once again.

There were footsteps followed by the sound of the unlatching of a chain. Then the door opened and Isabel was greeted by the sight of

Leo, wearing a pair of khaki shorts, but bare-chested. On his feet he had a pair of Moroccan slippers made of what looked like carpet material.

She was taken aback. "Oh . . . I . . ."

Leo laughed. "Hey, Isabel, come in. We were expecting somebody else."

Isabel wondered who that might be. Was this Leo's normal, minimalist garb when at home, even if visitors were expected?

She followed him into a large entrance hall. This was tidily kept, with a coat stand on one side, and on the other a couple of straight-backed dining-room chairs, a console table, and a Chinese ceramic umbrella vase into which a number of fly-fishing rods had been inserted.

"Cat's in the bath," said Leo. "She'll be out in a few minutes. Can I make you coffee?"

Isabel accepted, and Leo showed her into a large sitting room with windows overlooking the Meadows.

"Some view, hey?" said Leo. "That's the old Infirmary over there, and that's the university. And if you look over to that side, over there, you can see the Salisbury Crags. See them?"

Isabel looked, and nodded. "You get the northern light," she said.

"Light's light," said Leo. "I don't see much difference."

Isabel thought: Was someone like Leo susceptible to such things? "Northern light is colder," she said. "It's clearer too. Sharper. That's why artists prefer their studios to face north."

"Oh, yeah?"

"Yes. Have you been in the Art College? Have you seen those large studios they have on the northern side?"

Leo shook his mane of hair. "No. Never."

She had avoided looking at him directly, having been unprepared for his semi-nakedness. Now she glanced at him, at his powerful shoulders and muscular arms, at the abdomen that seemed, in this light, to be striated by lines of muscle just below the surface. She did not find him attractive: no muscle-bound male torso appealed to her. But she saw how, according to one aesthetic at least, he was the perfect specimen. And of course he was like a lion: this was how a lion looked from the side—smooth, muscled flanks, powerful, rippling, ready to spring.

She imagined for a moment what it would be like to hold him. It would be like embracing something powerful and dangerous—something that would suddenly overpower you, unleash a hidden, overwhelming force.

He was looking at her. "Excuse my undress," he said, smiling—provocatively, she thought. "In the flat, in this warm weather, we don't bother much. In fact, Cat and I often don't bother at all—it's rather comfortable walking round with nothing on."

Isabel turned away. She felt a physical revulsion at Leo's sheer animality. And she thought, reluctantly, of Leo and Cat prowling around—because that was how she imagined Leo moving—prowling around like two caged animals in this flat, naked, with Cat purring and Leo making that strange, growling sound that she imagined lions made when they breathed; that thought was so distasteful that she struggled to put it out of her mind. But we cannot **unthink,** she reminded herself; that was why psychologists had a whole category of "unwelcome" thoughts—thoughts, or images, that came into the mind unbidden and were the object of shame or distaste, even of horror.

"You don't approve," Leo suddenly said.

She spun round. Was he suggesting that she did not approve of **him**? She did not, of course, although that was the last thing she wanted to say. You could not tell people you disliked them—you might show it, but you could not say it.

Isabel struggled to respond. "Don't approve of what?"

"Of going round in the nude."

Isabel was immediately relieved. "Oh, that. I don't give it much thought," she said. "Some people like it—that's up to them."

"But you and Jamie," said Leo. "Do you ever wander around with no clothes on?"

Isabel fixed him with a stare. The intrusiveness of the question had shocked her. She was no prude, but she believed strongly that one did not talk about private matters of that sort. There were plenty of exhibitionists, of course—social media seemed to encourage people to lead their lives in public, even those parts of life that were conventionally private. But Isabel would never dream of asking anybody to reveal the secrets of the bedroom. For that is what they were—no matter how unsurprising or simply human they were, they fell into the category of the quintessentially personal. They were not to be paraded before others.

All she managed now was a curt "That's our affair."

Leo seemed unfazed by the brush-off. "You should try it," he said. "It's very liberating."

She noticed that he was looking down at his body as he spoke, pensively, as if reflecting on its merits.

Then he said, "I have very little body hair, you know. I mean, I have this big head of hair, but look at my chest—nothing. What's the thing in the Bible? Isn't it Jacob who says, 'My brother Esau is a hairy man, but I am a smooth man'? I always loved that. 'A hairy man!' I'm Jacob, I think—not Esau."

Isabel looked out of the window. She wondered when Cat was going to finish her bath, so that this intrusive, vaguely suggestive conversation with Leo could be brought to an end.

Her irritation got the better of her. "I don't like to talk about other people's body hair," she said. "Sorry, maybe I'm just old-fashioned.

Maybe that's the topic that most people talk about these days. Maybe I'm out of touch."

Leo liked that, and laughed. "Oh, that's great. No, they don't talk about it very much. Most people are still too uptight."

The word **uptight** stood out. It was some time since she had heard the word. She knew it had been popular once, in the late sixties and the seventies, at the time of the overturning of the old, stuffy world and its deadening conventions. You were uptight if you held on to the reservations of a more inhibited age. But people no longer seemed to say much about that.

"I haven't heard anybody say **uptight** recently," said Isabel. "You sound very old-fashioned, Leo. No offence, of course."

He defended himself. "I hear it all the time."

"Really?"

"Yes."

There came the sound of an opening door, and then Cat came into the room. She was wearing a bathrobe, and her hair, still wet, was slicked back. She seemed surprised, but not displeased, to see Isabel.

"Has Leo made you some of his legendary coffee?" she asked.

"He offered," said Isabel.

"I'm on my way," said Leo, making for the door to the kitchen.

Cat settled herself on a sofa and invited Isabel to join her. "I've been meaning to have you and Jamie round for ages," she said. "What do you think of my new flat?"

"I like it," said Isabel. "They're a good size, these places."

"Yes," said Cat. "But I suppose I'm going to have to get used to living on a boat. There's far less room, even on one of those big yachts."

"I'm sure you'll get used to it," Isabel said.

"Of course I'll keep this flat—for when I'm back in Edinburgh."

They talked about the move until Leo returned with coffee for Cat and Isabel. Isabel noticed that he had sweetened hers with vanilla syrup. The taste was cloying and unpleasant.

She looked at Cat and smiled. "I've come with a proposition," she said.

Cat's eyes widened. "I'm always interested in propositions."

"I wonder if you would consider selling the deli to the trust."

Cat sat back on the sofa, pulling a cushion onto her lap. "Hold on," she said. "Sell to Tweedledum and Tweedledee? To them?"

"To the trust," said Isabel. "Hamish and Gordon would do the legal bit, but it would be to the trust."

"Why?" asked Cat. "Why would the trust want to buy a deli?"

"As an investment," Isabel replied. "The trust already owns a lot of actual property—not just shares, but bricks and mortar. And besides, it would mean that Eddie's job would be secure. That's really why I'm suggesting it."

The mention of Eddie had an immediate effect. "That would be nice," said Cat. "I like Eddie."

"He's worked for you for years," said Isabel. "It would be good to do something for him."

Leo had been observing this; now he joined in. "Great idea," he said. "But a bit late, I'm afraid."

Isabel turned to face him. "Why too late? You haven't already sold it, have you?"

Cat was looking to Leo for the answer to

this. "Have we, Leo? I thought that the lawyer was waiting for Jonny's offer. I don't think it was in yet, was it?"

"First thing yesterday," said Leo. "It came in before ten. The lawyer phoned. Remember? We told him that he could accept it."

"Oh yes," said Cat. "I'd forgotten about that."

Isabel felt a wave of disappointment. "So it's all done and dusted?"

"Verbally," said Leo. "The lawyer was going to get the acceptance over to them in writing tomorrow, I think. He wanted to check up on something before he did that."

"So perhaps it's not too late," said Isabel.

Rather to her surprise, Cat rallied to her defence. "No, it may not be. If we haven't put it in writing, we can pull out, I think."

"But we told him," Leo protested. "I told Jonny—to his face—that he could have the place. I promised him."

Isabel saw Cat stiffen. "**You** told him? But I'm the owner, Leo—or I was, last time I looked at the deeds."

Leo was not to be put down. "Yeah, sure, but who's been doing the negotiation? Me.

Who organised the survey? Me. Who spoke to the agents? And so on."

"But it's my place," said Cat.

They stared at one another while Isabel, embarrassed but still secretly pleased by this sign of disagreement, looked on.

Cat turned to face Isabel. "I think we can get out of this deal with Jonny—as long as the trust can meet the price he's offered."

"We can," said Isabel. "Plus some, if necessary."

This caught Leo's attention. "Plus some? Plus how much?"

Isabel bit her lip. Leo's venality was so evident—surely Cat could notice it.

"Plus ten thousand," she said. She would square that with Hamish and Gordon; if there were any objection, then she would pay the extra from her own pocket.

Leo, who had been perched on a stool near the kitchen door, now rose to his feet and stood before the window, looking out. Isabel noticed the breadth of his shoulders, silhouetted against the sky. Cat saw her looking, and smiled conspiratorially. Isabel diverted her gaze.

"We can do that," said Leo. "I can phone the lawyer and tell him not to confirm."

"Good," said Cat. "And I'm quite pleased it's going to remain a delicatessen, and I'm pleased that Eddie can keep his job." She paused. "Poor Eddie."

"Nothing poor about him," muttered Leo, from the window. "He's a wimp—that's all."

Isabel looked at Cat. Her look said: Is this what you want?

Cat remained calm. "Eddie's not a wimp," she said to Leo. "He's vulnerable."

Leo made a dismissive noise.

"I mean it," said Cat. "Eddie was traumatised when he first came to work in the deli." She turned to Isabel. "You remember, Isabel? Remember what he was like?"

"Yes," said Isabel. "And he's made terrific progress. He's much happier now."

Leo snorted. "So he's traumatised . . . Who isn't? We all have stuff we carry with us— and we don't all let it turn us into snivelling wimps. Anyway, what happened? His father shouted at him? Some teacher was nasty about his homework?"

Isabel caught her breath. She watched Cat's reaction. It was not anger she saw, but a sort of resigned tolerance.

"Something shocking happened to Eddie," Cat said suddenly. "Do I have to spell it out, Leo?"

Leo's gaze seemed fixed on something outside. They waited, and eventually he said, "Well, those things happen. They just do."

Isabel wanted to intervene. She wanted to shake Leo, but she controlled herself. She said nothing. And Cat, she saw, was not going to do anything.

Cat broke the silence. "I'll phone the lawyer," she said to Isabel. "I'll ask him to speak to Hamish and Gordon. Will that do?"

"It will," said Isabel.

She leaned across the sofa, took Cat's hand and pressed it gently. "Thank you," she said.

She moved towards the door. Leo was still staring out of the window. She did not say goodbye to him, but once out of the door regretted that and came back in to do so. He did not seem to hear her, and she left it at that, but at least she had done what comity required.

SHE WALKED HOME across the Bruntsfield Links. Passing the local newsagent, she bought a copy of that day's **Scotsman,** the latest issue of the **London Review of Books** and a copy of **Edinburgh Life.** This was a glossy magazine that featured events and places around Edinburgh. Isabel enjoyed the social pages at the back—a record of charity balls and drinks parties in the form of photographs of people smiling at the camera. She recognised the same faces in many of the pictures— tireless attendees who went from one function to another, bravely appearing to enjoy themselves. We are such a social species, Isabel thought; it doesn't really matter what the occasion—we are a species that likes to cluster together for shelter, just as we did all those ages ago, in our caves, while creatures larger and stronger than ourselves prowled about outside. We liked company, and fire, and the warmth that both gave.

With the boys due to be collected from school and from playgroup in just over an hour's time, Isabel could not settle to anything.

Grace was tackling a pile of ironing upstairs—Isabel heard the sound of a podcast drifting down from the laundry room. Grace listened to podcasts when she ironed and could sometimes be heard volubly disagreeing with the speaker. Isabel felt unsettled: the meeting with Cat had gone as smoothly as she could have hoped—at least in that Cat seemed immediately to have been attracted by the idea of selling the deli to the trust. There was still the issue of Jonny Mustique's offer, but if Cat's understanding of the position was correct, then that did not threaten to be a major stumbling block. Everybody knew that contracts relating to land and building had to be in writing—at least in Scots law—and until that was done, nothing was definite. But the thought occurred to her that what she had done, perhaps unwittingly, was to have gazumped the hairdresser by offering more than the price he had agreed with Leo. On the other hand, it was Cat's business, not Leo's, and if Cat decided that she wanted a deal with a family trust—especially one that promised to look after her young employee—then that surely was her prerogative.

Isabel went into the kitchen to make herself a cup of tea. She was thinking of Leo, and she felt flustered and annoyed. His conversation with her had been an uncomfortable one in so many respects, straying, she thought, into that territory of unease that accompanies sexual suggestiveness. There were some men who took pleasure in testing a woman's sense of the private. They made allusions which, although innocent on the face of it, nonetheless pointed in a sexual direction. The entire tenor of her encounter with Leo had been like that, starting with semi-nakedness. There was exposure of the body, and then there was exposure of the body: a man might be bare-chested on the beach without any innuendo; in another setting, though, there could be an inference of intimacy—an invitation to look. What Leo should have done was to put on a shirt when she arrived; he had not. And then, when he had talked about wandering around the flat naked, he had effectively invited Isabel into a sexual confidence. And then, on top of all that, there had been the gross insensitivity of his remarks about Eddie.

Isabel felt dirtied by the whole experience.

Leo was crude. He was exactly the sort of man whom women were now determined to expose—the sort who thought he could get away with sexual imposition. And, thought Isabel, I am his fiancée's **aunt.** If he was like that with an aunt, even one not all that much older than he was, then what would he be like with some more vulnerable younger woman?

She tried to put him out of her mind while she waited for the kettle to boil. Then Grace came in, carrying a plastic washing basket stacked high with neatly ironed tea towels and tablecloths.

"I didn't hear you," said Grace. "I was upstairs."

"I heard your podcast," said Isabel.

Grace put the basket down on the table. "Did you hear what he said?"

Isabel shook her head. "No, I didn't. Who was it?"

"I don't know," Grace answered. "They gave his name at the beginning, but I didn't hear it. He was either Irish or American—I couldn't tell which. He might have been both, of course."

"And the subject?" asked Isabel.

"It was all about psychopaths," said Grace. "This fellow—the speaker—was some sort of doctor; a psychiatrist, I think. He looks after loonies."

Isabel smiled. "They're not loonies any longer, Grace. I don't think they use that term."

"Well, they sound like loonies to me," she said. "Crazies, then."

"I don't think they say that either."

"Well, whatever they say, he deals with them. And he knows a lot about what makes them tick. He says that you can X-ray their brains these days and see what's going on inside. Bits light up, apparently, and they can tell what's going on."

"Imaging," said Isabel.

"You know about the London taxi drivers and their enlarged brains?" Grace asked. "He mentioned that. He said that they've discovered that London taxi drivers, who have to spend three years studying the best way from A to B, have enlarged hippo . . ."

"Hippocampuses."

"That's it. And it's the same with psychopaths—not their hippocampuses, of course, but other bits where we keep our feelings—empathy, he said. Apparently, a psychopath doesn't have the same ability to feel empathy that we have. They can prove it now by doing a brain scan."

Isabel said that she thought that would make it easier for psychiatrists to be certain.

"Yes," said Grace. "But would you go in for a test like that? How would you feel?"

"I suppose it would depend on whether you thought you were a possible psychopath or not. I suspect that I'm not, thank goodness. And you aren't either."

Grace began to stack the tea towels in a drawer. "Do you know any?" she asked.

"Psychopaths?"

"Yes. Do you know anybody who's definitely a psychopath?"

Isabel tried to remember what she had read about the incidence of psychopathy. Was it two per cent of the population? It was something like that, she thought. Statistically, everyone would know at least one.

She thought of Professor Lettuce. He had some of the attributes of the psychopath—the cunning, the lack of empathy, the indifference to others. And yet he had lasting friendships, which psychopaths tended not to have. He was loyal to Christopher Dove, as Dove was loyal to him. Mind you, Dove was another potential psychopath—perhaps he and Lettuce were psychopaths together, drawn to one another by their particular psychopathology.

And then she thought of Leo. Yes! She remembered the incident with the champagne cork and Eddie's eye. Surely a normal person would have been alarmed—and regretful—when he saw that he had hit somebody in the eye with a cork. And there had been blood. Leo had seen all that, and yet his reaction had been to laugh. And then, only a few hours ago, he had described Eddie as a wimp, in a cold and unfeeling way. Surely that was psychopathic.

"Do you?" Grace pressed.

"I think I do," said Isabel.

"Who?" asked Grace.

"I may be wrong," said Isabel. "I shouldn't bandy names about if I may be wrong."

Grace picked up a tablecloth and started to refold it, holding one end of it under her chin. "I won't tell anybody else," she said. "You can tell me."

"I feel uncomfortable about it," said Isabel.

"Even though I know I can trust you." And she could: Grace understood confidentiality, and Isabel had never known her to tell anybody anything she had learned or seen in the house. It was innate.

"All right," said Isabel. "Leo. Cat's Leo."

Grace dropped the tablecloth. "Yes," she said, her voice lowered. "Him! You know something? While I was listening upstairs, I found myself thinking: That Leo—he's a psychopath if ever there was one. You can tell—you really can."

"I'm not sure we can be certain," said Isabel. "It's just a feeling—and we might be quite wrong."

"We aren't," said Grace. "Have you seen his eyes? They're that odd yellow colour—or maybe yellow isn't the right word . . . tawny, perhaps. They're that colour. Just like a lion's eyes."

"Yes, but—"

"And the way he looks at you," Grace continued. "As if sizing you up. Have you noticed that?"

"I suppose I have."

Grace shook her head sadly. "Cat had

better watch out. And now she's gone and got engaged to him. Can you believe it? Getting engaged to a man like that."

"She seems happy," said Isabel.

"So do lots of women who marry men like that," retorted Grace. "They're happy because he gives them something they want, and then the scales fall from their eyes and they realise what they've ended up with."

"Possibly," said Isabel.

"Not possibly—definitely." Grace paused, before continuing with increased vigour: "Cat's going to live to regret this. Maybe not immediately, but sooner or later. Give it a year, maybe two. At the most."

Isabel did not contradict Grace, and for the next few minutes the two women were together in the kitchen in silence, and in the agreement that sometimes—though not always—lies behind silence.

CHAPTER THIRTEEN

❖

OVER THE NEXT TWO WEEKS, Isabel spoke to Hamish and Gordon virtually every day. As she had promised to do, Cat had been in touch with her own lawyer immediately after Isabel had raised the possibility of buying the deli. Leo had not attempted to dissuade her from reneging on the verbal undertaking he had given to the hairdresser Jonny Mustique, who had, anyway, appeared to have gone slightly cold on the project. "I think he was quite relieved to get out of it," Leo said to Cat. "Just goes to show, doesn't it? People say things they don't mean." To which Cat had added, "And mean things they don't say," but had not explored the implications of this neat inversion. Both she and Leo were happy with the arrangement, she because it enabled her to face Eddie—of whom she was fond— and he because he felt that he had obtained an extra ten thousand pounds from the trust. "They must have money coming out of their ears," he remarked to Cat. She, intoxicated by her feelings for this virile, leonine man, did not bother to think of the implications of this remark.

Hamish and Gordon took a close interest in the purchase of the deli. They picked over details of the inventory, scrutinised the accounts with the zeal of the forensic accountant and spent some time on plans for the future of the business. Hamish's wife, Hannah, who was interested in **charcuterie** and who made her own bacon from pork loin she obtained from the local butcher, volunteered to help behind the counter. For her part, Cat rapidly became detached from day-to-day tasks associated with the running of the deli, now leaving most decisions to Eddie or Isabel.

Eddie had initially almost panicked when told of what was planned. Cat and the deli were synonymous in his mind; she had always

been there, ever since he had first been engaged, and he found it difficult to contem-
plate carrying on without her.

"But who's going to do the ordering?"
he asked Isabel. "I don't know where things
come from. She gets them all. She talks on the
phone to these people, but I haven't got a clue
who they are."

Isabel was patient with him. "Their details
are all there, Eddie. And it's not complicated—
not really. Eggs come from the egg supplier
near Longniddry. We have their telephone
number on their invoices. I've spoken to them
already. They have plenty of eggs and will send
us whatever we want."

"And duck eggs?" challenged Eddie. "What
about duck eggs?"

"They come from a woman in Dalkeith.
Once again, if you look in the filing cabinet,
there's a folder named 'Duck Eggs.' Her invoices are in there."

"And cheese?" Eddie persisted. "Look at all
the different cheese. How do we know which
to get?"

"You know which ones sell, Eddie," said
Isabel. "You sell them yourself."

Gradually the level of the young man's in-security dropped, and he began to make decisions himself. Isabel encouraged him gently, and found a useful ally in Hannah.

"He's so lost, that poor boy," Hannah said to Isabel. "I know you shouldn't go around mothering young men, but that's what I want to do with him. I want to wrap my arms around him. I want to tell him not to worry so."

"That's exactly what you **should** do," urged Isabel. "Hold his hand."

Hannah was tactful, and Eddie seemed to flourish under her care. After ten days of the new regime, before the transaction had been finalised but when Cat had virtually stopped coming into the deli in the mornings, Isabel approached Hannah with her proposition.

"Could you manage this place?" she asked. "I mean not just now, but on a permanent basis?"

As it happened, Hannah was about to see their only child, a daughter, off to university at Stirling. Hamish was at the office all day, and had his country dancing. She was a member of a book club that met infrequently. She ran the house in Morningside with such efficiency that all domestic chores were done by nine-thirty each morning. The idea of a full-time job running a deli suited her perfectly, and she accepted.

Eddie was relieved. "I like that lady," he confessed to Isabel. "She keeps putting her arm around me, but I don't mind too much. I like her perfume."

"That's good, Eddie," said Isabel. "That's kind of you."

Hamish was pleased at his wife's decision. "Hannah has a great deal of energy," he said to Isabel. "And she has a good business head on her. She's very careful not to waste money. She's from Aberdeen, you know."

Isabel smiled. "They have that reputation, don't they?"

"They certainly do," said Hamish. "And it's well deserved. I don't know if I ever told you about my father's cousin, Laurence. He was from Aberdeen. He used to repair hot-water bottles with a bicycle-tube repair outfit when the rubber perished. He made one last thirty-three years."

"A very fine man," said Gordon. "Nowadays people just throw things away."

Within a couple of days, Hannah had transformed Cat's office. Large planning charts appeared on the walls; ancient invoices were disposed of; boxes of superior latex gloves—with adequate talcum powder—were ordered, along with a whole set of personalised aprons on which the name of the deli was prominently printed. A blue-striped cap was ordered for Eddie, and he wore this at a jaunty angle. Four different types of bacon replaced the previous single variety; trays of large cheese scones, baked by Hannah herself, were placed temptingly on the counter and sold out within hours.

Jamie was pleased to see that the prospect of Isabel having to devote large amounts of time to the deli had receded. He got on well with Hannah, whom he thought was an inspired choice for the job. He delighted in Eddie's happiness, which was overt, and infectious.

"This is going to be really good," Eddie said.

"Yes," said Isabel. "And we want to make you assistant manager. Hannah's going to be manager—but you will be her assistant."

This took a while to sink in. Then he said, "Me? You mean me?"

"We mean you," said Isabel. "Gordon will draw up a new contract for you." She looked at him. She struggled to hold back the tears. "I'm really happy for you, Eddie. I know you're going to do this really well."

"Me?" he repeated. "Me?"

"Yes," she said. "You. Who else?"

CAT AND LEO married at a marina near Oban, the ceremony being performed by a licensed humanist officiant from Fort William, a woman who carried a small lapdog with her to every ceremony she conducted. They invited only a handful of people: the man who was installing solar panels on the new boat; Cat's friend Erica, from Birmingham; Leo's cousin, who worked for a brewery in Dublin; and his friend Stan, who was a pilot with a cheap airline. Isabel and Jamie were sent photographs of the wedding itself, with Leo in a kilt and a rough green shirt that was laced rather than buttoned. Cat wore a sleek dress of brown Thai silk. The celebrant had her lapdog under her arm and Stan was in his pilot's uniform.

"Bizarre," said Isabel.

"Seriously funny" was Jamie's verdict. "Do you think she's happy?"

Isabel considered her answer. "I think she is," she said. "She adores him."

"But what does she see in him?"

Isabel sighed. "The usual thing," she said. She did not want to elaborate. The happiness of others was often inexplicable. People got by; people sought different things; they felt their way through the accidental circumstances of their lives. They snatched at small scraps of happiness which, sometimes to the surprise of others, were enough.

A MONTH after the purchase of the deli, Isabel was in La Barantine one morning, drinking a cup of coffee before returning to the house and a day of unremitting editorial activities. The solstice had passed, and the summer had ripened. It was almost time for the Festival to begin, and the city was filling with artistic visitors. As Isabel sat in her window seat, she watched a group of very obvious students walk past. They had university drama group stamped all over them, and they were in Edinburgh for the Fringe. She could not help but smile. They would be putting on something by Beckett, or **West Side Story,** or a new and troubling play by one of their own number. They would spend several weeks sleeping on somebody's floor or, if they were lucky, on their couch. They would have tiny audiences and they would lose whatever money they had. They would be blissfully happy—immortal; talented beyond the world's understanding; inhabitants of a moment, and a stage, made just for them.

Isabel turned to her newspaper. There was a small war somewhere, getting worse. There were people adrift on the sea, desperate for somewhere—anywhere—to land. There was nothing new.

She looked up. A woman had come into the café and was standing before her. It was Hilary Reay.

"Do you mind?" said Hilary. "You seem absorbed."

Isabel felt her heart beating hard within her. She was nervous. "No, not at all."

Hilary drew up a chair. "The town's getting crowded. Have you noticed?"

Isabel glanced through the window. She was thinking. Did Hilary know about the conversation she and Jamie had had with Iain? Was this going to be a confrontation?

Hilary fiddled with the menu. "Iain hasn't been that well," she said. "Had you heard?"

Isabel shook her head. "I'm sorry."

"He's being so brave about it," said Hilary. "But, in a way, I suppose he has everything sorted out. There are no loose ends for him."

Isabel said nothing. She was waiting.

"He told us that you were no longer going to be the executor."

Isabel inclined her head. "I was rather over-extended. I have a lot on."

"Oh, I understand," said Hilary. "I understand perfectly. And, anyway, he sorted things out, as I expect you may know."

Isabel shook her head. "I don't, I'm afraid."

"He made arrangements for the estate to be shared by the three families," she said. "He never really wanted that, he said, but he saw no alternative."

"Perhaps that was the best solution," said Isabel. She felt a flood of relief. Hilary did not know of the part they might have played in turning Iain against her.

There was a further surprise. "No, I don't think it was the only option. Jack felt that he couldn't take it on—and I agreed with him. And Sarah was lukewarm too. The only one who could do it was John. So we made over our interest to him—with Iain's agreement—and he's getting stuck in."

Isabel said nothing. She looked away. She had to say something, because she could not leave matters as they were. It might not be wise, but she decided to do it.

She turned to face Hilary. "Years ago, you know, I saw you."

Hilary frowned. "Years ago? When . . ."

"Yes, when we were both on jury duty. But then I saw you a few months later, right here—in this very café."

Hilary still looked puzzled. "So? So you saw me?"

"You were with that man. That man Macglashian."

Isabel watched the effect of her words.

"And then," she continued, "you went outside—with him—and I saw you shake hands with him."

"It's a long time ago . . ."

"Yes," said Isabel. "A long time. But it stuck in my mind, you see, because you had just been one of the people who wanted to acquit him. You knew him, didn't you? You sat on that jury in the knowledge that you should not be there. And you argued for his acquittal—in spite of all the evidence against him, you wanted him acquitted."

Hilary sat quite still. Her mouth was slightly open, as if she had been caught unawares. Then she shook her head very slowly. "No, no. It wasn't like that. It wasn't."

Isabel shook her head. "Well, if you'll forgive me, I can't see how it can be interpreted in any other way. You were on a jury that acquitted somebody you knew. I heard you argue for acquittal. You were the main voice raised for that verdict. A short time afterwards, I saw you in the street with the man you wanted acquitted."

"There's a small matter of evidence," said Hilary. "You don't convict somebody just because you don't like the look of him." She looked at Isabel accusingly, as if to suggest that this was what had been behind Isabel's desire to convict.

"If you think that was what I did," began Isabel. "Then—"

Hilary stopped her. "I didn't say you did."

"You implied it," said Isabel, her tone coldly polite. "And there was a lot of evidence, you know. I listened to that, just as you must have done . . . Or maybe we heard different things."

Isabel waited.

Hilary was staring at her. "You don't believe me, do you?"

The directness of the accusation upset Isabel. It was one thing to express scepticism about what somebody was saying; it was another thing altogether to make a direct accusation of mendacity. She hesitated. Suddenly, Hilary looked truthful to her. She was not sure why, but it was something in her expression. Liars, she thought, don't look like this.

"I wouldn't say that," Isabel muttered.

Hilary continued to look directly at Isabel. There was no flinching; there was no sliding away of looks. "I didn't know him before the trial. I didn't."

Isabel raised an objection, but she was changing her mind, and the objection sounded tame. "So what were you doing talking to him then? And your husband too? What was he doing?"

"Macglashian was on the board of a small museum in Glasgow. They kept him on after the trial—he had given them a lot. They were buying one of Jack's pictures. At that time, I handled all of Jack's sales. I was making all the arrangements."

Isabel stared at her. "You're telling me it was a business meeting?"

"Yes. It was."

"And your arguing that he was innocent. That had nothing to do with it?" Isabel had now come round to the view that Hilary's story was entirely credible.

"I believed he was innocent. Or rather, I thought it **likely** that he was innocent. I wasn't sure, you see, and I felt if there was a doubt then we should be very careful about our verdict."

"So you were prepared to do business with him, afterwards?"

For the first time, Hilary raised her voice. "Yes! And doesn't it occur to you that it would be wrong to behave otherwise? If you're acquitted, the law says you're innocent, and you should be treated accordingly."

Isabel felt ashamed. "Yes," she said. "You should."

Hilary looked at her challengingly. "Well then."

Isabel's shame grew. "You sent me a picture."

Hilary nodded. "I did."

"I thought it was a bribe," said Isabel. "I'm sorry, but that's what I thought."

"It wasn't," said Hilary. "But do you know, after I sent it to you and I received no acknowledgement, it occurred to me that that was what you thought. I felt mortified. I lost sleep over it."

"I'm terribly sorry," said Isabel. "I've done you a real injustice."

Hilary hesitated. It was clear that she was hurt by Isabel's lack of trust, but she seemed to overcome that. She shook her head. "No, no. I'm immensely relieved that we've sorted this out. It felt all wrong to me—wrong and confused."

"I sold the picture," Isabel continued. "I sold it and gave the money to one of Macglashian's victims. I don't know if you remember her. She's the only one of the victims who gave evidence."

"The single mother? A hairdresser, wasn't she?"

"Yes, her."

"I've seen her from time to time," said Hilary. "She works in that salon on Morningside Road. I've seen her in the street." Suddenly, she laughed. "What a peculiar business— all round. What a complete... complete mess."

Isabel agreed. "But..."

"But sorted out," said Hilary. "By you. It never occurred to me to do anything to help that woman. It simply didn't occur."

"It just happened," said Isabel.

"So, would you like another cup of coffee?"

"Please," said Isabel. "I suspect that there's more to talk about."

"Probably," said Hilary. "That woman— so you had no trouble finding her?"

"I didn't."

"And you gave her the money."

"I did."

"Happy?"

"Ecstatic."

"Good."

Isabel waited a few moments; then she said, "You can be so wrong, can't you? About just about everything."

"As long as you aren't wrong **all** the time," said Hilary.

"Sometimes I feel I am," confessed Isabel.

"I suspect you're wrong about that," said Hilary, with a smile.

TWO DAYS LATER, at the Edinburgh Academy concert, Isabel sat by herself towards the back of the hall. Jamie, along with other members of the music staff, was busy arranging for the individual pupils to perform. Mark Brogan's slot came halfway through the programme, a bassoon solo by a French composer whom nobody had heard of, accompanied on the piano by Jamie. Mark made a false start, and they began again. Then, halfway through, he missed several bars, although Jamie was able quickly to work out where he was and resume his accompaniment. There were stifled giggles from two rows of fellow students at the front, quickly smothered by a stern glance from the rector and his wife. Mark's parents sat in the middle of the third row, beaming with pleasure and pride. A small boy, seated just behind them, nudged his friend, pointed at Mrs. Brogan and whispered, "Jeez, look at her hair. Cosmic."

As was usually the case with the weaker players, the applause that greeted Mark's completion of his piece was deafening. Neither of his parents suspected that the clapping was ironic; they felt too elated to make such a fine judgement.

Back at the house, where Grace, doing a sleepover babysit, had already retired to her room, Jamie and Isabel sat in the kitchen and shared the last glass of wine from a bottle they found in the fridge. There were several books on the kitchen table: Jamie had been at a book sale and had come home with a book of poetry, a biography of Patrick Leigh Fermor, and a book on the Darien colony—Scotland's Central American disaster.

He picked up the book of poetry. "Have you seen this?" he said to Isabel. "Scottish poetry. There are woodcuts. Look at this one. Celtic."

He opened the book at random and found what he was looking for. Three figures, in a typical Celtic circle, held hands with one another, arms in a complicated pattern of intermingling. "I love that," he said. "I think it says everything there is to be said about helping one another and loving one another and being part of . . . well, I suppose being part of something bigger than oneself."

Isabel looked. "The geometry of holding hands," she said.

She reached out and took his hand, the hand of the man she loved beyond any expression of love, and who reciprocated that love, every moment of it, every atom, every contour, every echo.

ABOUT THE AUTHOR

Alexander McCall Smith is the author of the No. 1 Ladies' Detective Agency novels and of a number of other series and stand-alone books. His works have been translated into more than forty languages and have been best sellers throughout the world. He lives in Scotland.

LIKE WHAT YOU'VE READ?

Try these titles by Alexander McCall Smith,
also available in large print:

**The Second-Worst
Restaurant in France**
ISBN 978-1-9848-9043-6

The Talented Mr. Varg
ISBN 978-0-593-17204-9

**The Department
of Sensitive Crimes**
ISBN 978-1-9848-4738-6

For more information on large print titles, visit
www.penguinrandomhouse.com/large-print-format-books